W9-BHN-729

A High and Hidden Place

A HIGH AND HIDDEN PLACE

A NOVEL

Michele Claire Lucas

HarperSanFrancisco
A Division of HarperCollins*Publishers*

F LUCAS

HarperCollins books may be purchased for educational, business, or sales promotional use. For information please write: Special Markets Department, HarperCollins Publishers, Inc., 10 East 53rd Street, New York, NY 10022.

HarperCollins Web site: http://www.harpercollins.com

HarperCollins®, 🏭 ®, and HarperSanFrancisco™ are trademarks of Harper-Collins Publishers, Inc.

FIRST EDITION

Library of Congress Cataloging-in-Publication Data

Lucas, Michele Claire.
    A high and hidden place : a novel / Michele Claire Lucas. — 1st ed.
        p. cm.
    ISBN 0–06–074056–6 (cloth)
    I. Title.
PS3612.U24H54   2005
813'.6—dc22   2004054060

05 06 07 08 09 RRD(H) 10 9 8 7 6 5 4 3 2 1

In memory of my father, Fred Lucas,
a patron of the arts

In memory of my mother, Claire Lucas,
who filled my childhood with her music

For Alexandra and James and Owen Daniel Molloy
who are the best part of my own story

ORA' DOUR

Latin for *Place of Prayer.*

Photograph reprinted by courtesy of Collection Ribiere/Sipa.

How long, O Lord, will you hide yourself forever?

—PSALM 89:46

*Not that I am (I think) in much danger of ceasing
to believe in God. The real danger is coming to
believe such dreadful things about Him. The conclusion I dread
is not "So there's no God after all," but "So this is what God's
really like. Deceive yourself no longer."*

—C. S. LEWIS, *A Grief Observed*

A High and
Hidden place

PROLOGUE

"Reverend Mother, this is Christine Lenoir," the lady with the funny hat and the frowning face says to the angel, "the child I told you about, the one from Oradour."

The halo all about the angel's face shines in the darkness. Maman told me of the angels, that they are all about to help us when we are scared. I am very scared, and here she is.

"Ah, yes, Christine Lenoir of Oradour," the angel says. She kneels in front of me and puts her hand against my cheek. "Little Christine of Oradour, I am so happy you have come. We have been waiting for you."

They have been waiting for me. I look into the angel's face, so close to mine, and I'm not scared anymore. I'm not sure what to call an angel come to earth, so I say, "Bonsoir, Madame."

The woman at my side says, "Bonsoir, *Mother*," and I jump she sounds so angry. She should not speak in such a mean way in front of an angel.

"She is not my mother."

"She is a holy mother of this house of God," the lady says as she squeezes my hand hard until it hurts.

"Come, little Christine of Oradour, come," the angel mother says. She smiles at me and her face is kind and beautiful. She takes my hand from the lady I do not like, and the angel mother's hand around mine feels cool and gentle. She looks down on me and I love her. I love her as much as I love my guardian angel. More. I love the angel mother more, for I can see her and touch her. Of course, I do not love her as I love Maman who is from the earth. Maman went off somewhere, and my papa, and my two brothers, and my grandpapas, and my grandmamans, and my aunts and uncles and cousins all went with her. An outing in the country, it was such a fine day. Maman left me behind because she could not find me. I went to the woods when she told me not to, and she didn't know where my secret hiding place was, behind a big rock. But I do not understand where they are now. It is dark and cold outside. They should be home by now. I wanted to wait in my house for Maman to come back, but the mean lady took me away even though I cried and cried and hit her on the arm. Now I understand why she brought me to this place to wait for Maman, because she knew with the angel I wouldn't be scared. And I'm not. I know Maman will come for me. Even though I was naughty yesterday before she left, she never stays cross with me for long. Maman will return to take me home. I am her only little girl. I am her happiness. She has often told me so. I'm worried though, because she'll look for me at our house and I won't be there. I'll ask the angel mother about this. She'll know.

The angel mother's shoes don't make any noise as we walk a hallway, dark and long. My wooden shoes are making awful clumping sounds for I have to hurry to keep up. The floor creaks, a sound like my own house makes, my house in Oradour. I can lie in bed at night and know where Maman and Papa are by the creaking of the floors—the parlor, the hallway, the little room under the stairs where Papa reads—for the floor in each place makes a different sound, a tiny sound, but I can tell. The best is the squeak of the stairs, for then I know that Maman and Papa are coming up to bed, that they will be in the room just next to mine.

I am close at the angel mother's side. Her long robe smells like church. The beads that hang from her waist touch my face, and the big silver cross hanging from her neck so everyone will know she is an angel of the Lord Jesus swings a little as we go. I don't know where we are going, but I hope she is taking me to Maman. Maybe there's going to be a surprise party for my First Communion.

We come to a stop and the angel mother opens up a big wooden door. I am hoping for cake and ice cream and all my family calling out, "Surprise!" But all there is is the biggest room I have ever seen and it is full of beds. Other little girls are all about, but there is to be no party, I can see that at once, for they are wearing nightdresses. These must be the angel mother's children, angel children. I am so sad that my family is not here, I think I am going to cry. But I try very hard not to, and I squeeze my eyes to hold in the tears.

"You must be tired," the angel mother says, and I am, very tired. She must be tired too, having so many children to care for.

"This is Christine of Oradour," she says to her children as we walk the little path between the beds. "She has come to stay with us. God has brought her to us by his grace and we must make her feel welcome."

We stop at a bed and the angel mother tells me to sit beside her. "You must not be afraid, Christine. You will be safe with us."

"Yes, Angel Mother."

"My name is Mother Céline. I know you are upset and confused, but you see, God has taken your family to be with Him in Paradise, and so it is given to me and to the others here to care for you and raise you to be God's child."

"Yes, Angel Mother Céline."

She smiles. "No, no, just Mother Céline. You must call me Mother Céline."

"Yes, Mother Céline."

"There now, that's fine. Are you hungry?"

"No, Mother Céline."

"Perhaps a little bread and jam, a glass of milk?"

"Does my mother know where I am?"

"Oh, yes, she knows. And she is happy that you are in a safe and holy place."

"She will know where to find me?"

"Christine, when you go to Paradise that is where you remain for eternity. Someday when you too go to Paradise, you will see your mother there. But she will not come back to earth again, my child."

"I am *not* your child. My mother will so come back for me, you'll see that she will. She didn't go to Paradise. She just went on a country outing." This must be a terrible sin, talking back to an angel, but I can't let her think that Maman will not come for me. "My mother will come and she will take me back to Oradour. She will. We have a fine house there, and Papa has his pharmacy and Maman has her garden. I have a dog. His name is Toby. He will be looking for me. We'll go back to Oradour very soon, tomorrow, you'll see." I thought angels knew everything, but I must be wrong. Maybe only God and the Blessed Mother know everything.

"We'll talk of this again in the morning, when you have had a good sleep. Now, there is a clean nightdress under the pillow. Put it on and I shall bring you something to eat."

I don't want the other little girls to see my body, so I hide myself within the nightdress before I take off the dress that was given to me to wear for the journey. It is too big and makes me feel ashamed. I let it drop to the floor, I step out of it and leave it right there. This is naughty, but I don't care. I want my own clothes, the clothes Maman made for me that fit me just right. I know I should not be bad in a house of angels, so I pick up the dress and put it on the bed.

The other little girls are whispering, giggling behind their hands. I guess angel children can be naughty too, talking behind my back about Christine of Oradour as everyone has called me since Maman went away. Christine of Oradour, everyone says, as though the town where I come from is part of my name, like Francis of Assisi or Thérèse of Lisieux. But I am not a saint. If that's what people think, they are wrong. I was a naughty girl who disobeyed her mother and so was left behind when everyone went to the country. But Maman will come for me. She'll take me back to Oradour and everything will be as before.

The angel mother brings me a tray. I eat a little, to please her, but I am too tired to be hungry. The milk is good, cool and soft going down my throat, and she is happy when I drink it all down.

She takes me to the bathroom. I can't go with her in the room even though I have to badly, but she leaves to fetch a towel and then I can. When she comes back, I wash my face and hands. She gives me a towel but it's not soft like Maman's towels. I wonder why.

The angel mother tucks me in as Maman always does. "There now, Christine, it is time for rest in order to be ready for the new day," she says. Her face is close to mine and she kisses my cheeks. The halo all about her face feels hard against my skin. I thought it would be soft but it is stiff and scratchy, like the towel. The angel mother smells like soap and like the wind.

"Say your prayers and thank the Lord Jesus for bringing you here to us, and I shall thank Him too for such a blessing. Mother Agnès will be watching over you during the night. She will be at the desk right by the door, you see? If you want anything you just ask her. If you need to go to the bathroom in the night, Mother Agnès will take you. Now sleep, for you will be safe."

Another angel mother from God. I know I will be safe here until Maman comes for me. I don't know why she is so late. We have to get ready for the First Communion tomorrow. Or is it the next day? I don't know. The days are all mixed up now. It must be the next day because Maman and I have a lot to do and Maman wouldn't forget about that. We have to pick flowers from the garden to put on the altar, and some herbs for the sandwiches. And Maman has to bake a cake. I'm to help her. She puts everything in a big bowl and then I stir. And we have to make the little sandwiches. It will be a grand party. Yes, Maman will be here tomorrow, first thing, I'm sure of that. Mustn't worry. Maman wouldn't forget about my First Holy Communion of all things. She made me a beautiful dress. It will be the prettiest of all.

Before I fall asleep, I ask the Lord Jesus to forgive me for disobeying my mother. I ask Him to show Maman the way to this place where I am so she won't get lost.

I was brought, at the age of six, to a convent, a cloistered place of asylum from the world that was roiling and thundering and awash in blood. I did not know then, of course, that the whole world was teeming with the motherless, the fatherless, the homeless, the dispossessed. I did not know then that I was an orphan among orphans, one of so many everywhere in the world, made so by events beyond my sight, beyond my awareness, in any case beyond my six-year-old ability to comprehend.

The angel mothers were, in truth, nuns of the Sacred Heart of Jesus, a teaching order of scholarly women dedicated to the education, temporal and spiritual, of young girls. War had demanded an enlargement of their vocation to include the care and upbringing of girl children orphaned by man's brutality as I had been, and had made of them mothers indeed. I came to understand, of course, that these women who nurtured me and educated me and loved me were not angels, but they were as holy and as kind and as full of grace as any angel might have been, and I loved them as my family, as much as my own blood kin. In fact, I soon enough forgot my mother and the rest of my family. They had disappeared from my sight in a day, and then gradually, with the months and then the years, from my mind and my heart. The angel mothers became my parents, the other orphan girls, who were indeed no angel children after all, became my siblings. It may be difficult to believe, but my childhood, both before and after the terrible day of fire, was a very happy one. But though I did not know it, I would forevermore be Christine of Oradour, with all that that appellation implied.

PARIS, 1964

1

It was early morning. I walked, as I did each day at this time, along the small market street just around the corner from my apartment. As I went along, from butcher shop to bakery to greengrocer, I filled my string bag with the provisions I would need for the day. I had already bought a small bifteck, a bunch of carrots, a baguette, a pint of milk. It remained only to stop at the patisserie for a piece of my favorite almond cake, a dessert for my evening meal.

I already knew the shopkeepers on the street. They greeted me warmly and called me by name even though I had only been living in the neighborhood for a few months. My small apartment did not have an ice box, and so I shopped each day along with the housewives of the quartier, which was the usual way at this time, even for those who possessed modern appliances. I enjoyed making my early morning rounds, choosing my provisions, planning my day as well as my meals as I went along. I enjoyed the camaraderie with the merchants, the other shoppers, the same women each day. I looked forward to their friendly smiles, the tidbits of neighborhood gossip, the inquiries as to my health and well-being. It was as though I were a member of a small country community and not just an anonymous resident in a big city. A newcomer, the local residents always made me feel as though I belonged.

I had recently spent a year in New York at the main office of the news magazine for which I worked, and then I had returned to France and to my job at the Paris bureau of *World* magazine.

I loved my new home, on the top floor of an old building at 18, avenue de la Motte Picquet, on the Left Bank near Les Invalides. Motte Picquet was a fine, wide boulevard lined with chestnut trees and old buildings, many with grand facades featuring ornate stonework and fancy wrought-iron railings around their verandahs. At the corner was a friendly, cheerful bistro where I felt comfortable eating alone and where, soon enough, the waiters knew my name as I knew theirs. They always remembered what I had been willing to tell them about my life, and they loved to hear the latest goings-on at the famous news magazine where I worked. In the middle of the block was a small cinema that showed older French as well as foreign films, and, of course, just off the boulevard was the street lined with shops that I traversed each day. At the end of this street was a small neighborhood church, which I had never entered.

The apartment itself was a quirky place, for it was an apartment within an apartment. My small rooms—a sitting room, a bedroom, a tiny kitchen and a bathroom— had been made out of one corner of a spacious flat that belonged to a famous singer, Monsieur Pierre Bernac. I entered by the main door into a large entrance hallway, then turned right toward the door leading to my sitting room. To the left were Monsieur Bernac's rooms. The only one I had been permitted to see was a spacious library with overstuffed furniture and a grand piano. It was here that the singer, retired now from performing himself, gave lessons to a select group of students who came from all over the world to study with him, so great was his reputation. It was in this wonderful room that the tall, imperious man had interviewed me, with great seriousness, great intensity, about my qualifications for living under his roof. I had to assure him that I intended to live alone, that I was a quiet person, that I did not give parties, and that I led a sober existence. My references from my convent school and university and employer probably reassured him as to my character and lifestyle, but there must have been residual doubts about a single young woman, for when he gave over the keys to his front door and to my own, he shook his head as though he thought he was making a serious mistake. Each time I passed him, coming or going, he greeted me politely if formally, but always with a dubious expression as though he suspected I had a man stashed behind my door with whom I was planning raucous parties.

One of the pleasures of my new home was the wonderful music, splendid arias and lyrical songs, that wafted from the library just adjacent to my bedroom. The students were all male, with wonderful, rich voices, and it was as though private concerts had been included in my rent. I had been told by the wine merchant on the street where I shopped that Monsieur Bernac was—he whispered the words—a homosexual. Living within the confines of a homosexual's private world was somehow exciting to me, as though I were part of a decadent way of life. I had to suppose that Monsieur Bernac's students were not necessarily of their teacher's sexual persuasion, but I couldn't help looking at the young men coming and going and wondering which one might be the great man's lover, or perhaps which ones, since I judged the life of a homosexual male to be a promiscuous one. Of course, I had no knowledge on which to base such an assumption.

I was grateful to be back in France after my year in New York. It was an interesting experience working there and I had learned a lot about my profession. But the hectic pace had worn me out and some of the people with whom I worked were harsh and foul-mouthed and disagreeable. Not everyone of course. I had met one nice man about my own age who wrote for the science and medical sections of the magazine, and he had made my time in New York more tolerable. But on the whole I didn't have much in common with the people in New York. I was glad to have had the opportunity to see America and to grow in my work, but, in truth, I was happy to be back in my homeland. I wanted to be in a place where I felt truly comfortable, where life was familiar and comprehensible. I was exhausted and, for the time being, I didn't have the strength or resilience to negotiate a foreign culture.

It was foolish of me, for my work at the magazine kept me on the run, but I enrolled in a history course at the Sorbonne on France from 1930 to 1945. I was no longer interested in the ancient world, the Middle Ages, and the Renaissance, as I had been when I was a university student. I wanted now to study more recent times, the events that had led to a war during my own lifetime in which thousands of my countrymen had been killed. I wanted to learn all I could about the forces that had led to such disaster, and about events that, I had recently discovered, affected me so personally. It was odd to think that the time of my childhood was already considered historical, especially since I was only twenty-six years old, and that a whole curriculum in the history department at the Sorbonne had been created to cover these years, not just in France but around the world.

Of course I had not realized when I was a little girl what was happening outside my convent home. I had not known about the doctor and the retired schoolteacher in the nearby town of Fontvielle who had been taken away to a concentration camp never to return. I had not realized that the little girl who had stayed at the convent for a few days and then was gone as suddenly as she had arrived had been fleeing people who would have her dead. I had not known about the bombs falling on cities, the fighting to the north and south of where I lived, the deadly reprisals that had been exacted against civilian populations by the enemy. I had not known that children just like me were dying in bombing raids or in gas chambers or of starvation. I had lived a protected, peaceful existence during a time that was now considered to be the bloodiest and the most tragic in human history. I felt compelled to learn about what had happened all around me, near and far, as I had innocently gone about my childhood—attending my classes, doing my lessons, playing with my sisters, reading my storybooks, eating my nutritious meals—without even being aware of how others were suffering all around the world. I felt compelled to learn about these events, not just because everyone should possess such knowledge, but because a small part of that history, I now knew, was my own personal story.

My work and my studies kept me very busy, as I intended. I didn't want time to think too much, to remember too much, to imagine too much. I was up early each morning, I went to bed late, and I slept hard. The dreams that had for the last few months intruded on my rest, nudging fragmented pieces of the past into my awareness, went dark, and I arose each morning with no more knowledge of my own story within the history I was studying than I had taken to bed with me the night before. I was grateful for the respite. I had already learned more about that small event than I wanted to know.

As I became more and more engrossed in the course I was taking, I became more and more dissatisfied with my work at *World* Inc. I was bored with my assignments, cranky with my coworkers, testy and adversarial with my editors. As the weeks went by, I became certain about the direction I wanted to take in my life, and one day, armed with this conviction, I abruptly terminated my job at *World*. I had decided that journalism was not for me. I didn't have the right disposition for intruding on other people's lives, asking inane questions of those in tragic circumstances, pushing myself into places where I was not wanted. I wasn't aggressive enough to be a journalist, which was probably the reason I had been so unhappy in New York. It wasn't the American people I disliked, it was the journalists, of whatever nationality, necessarily assertive and bombastic by nature and training, who made me uncomfortable. I had made a terrible career choice, one not suited to my temperament and my inclinations. History would be my vocation, a particular history of a particular time. It would be difficult to switch gears. Money would be tight and I would have to do freelance editing and translation work while I studied for my degree. But suddenly I felt completely free for the first time in my life, free to do as I chose without regard to anyone else's opinion or expectations, and I was certain that I was at last on the right course in my life.

"Christine, over here, over here!"

Sophie was waving madly at me from her position on the steps. A more prompt person than I, she always tried to save me a seat in the big lecture hall, but today she had only managed a little space on the steps between the rows. There were more students for the course on Germany than space allowed. It seemed I was one among many interested in the recent past, and the professor had a reputation for being both learned and entertaining.

I had met Sophie Hahn on the very first day of the winter term when I enrolled as a full-time student, and we had become fast friends almost at once. She was an edgy, intense young woman with a massive amount of red, curly hair that I could spot easily among the crowds of students. She was always agitated about one thing or another, her obsessions changed almost daily, but she had a wonderful sense of humor as well, and even on my most down days, she could always make me laugh. I squeezed myself next to her on the step.

"My God, you just can't be on time."

"I'm sorry. I had to finish that translation for Monsieur Monsard. It was terribly difficult."

"You don't want to miss any of this lecture, Christine. Today is the day we meet Adolph Hitler."

I shivered. I suddenly wasn't certain I was ready to come face to face with evil.

"Well, what did you think about the lecture?"

"It was fascinating. This is what I want to learn about. I want to learn everything I can. At the same time, it is difficult to contemplate the nature of evil, to face it square on," I said.

"But we must, I believe. We absolutely must."

Sophie and I were sitting in our favorite student café, hunched over our steaming cups of coffee. If we could manage it, we always came here after class. Sophie was even busier than I was. She had a job in a bookstore and she cared for her sister who was not well. In what way Steffa was not well Sophie never said, and I never asked, not wanting to intrude on private realms. Still, I always asked after Steffa, and the answers were always much the same. "Steffa is better today," Sophie would say, or "Steffa is having a spell today," or "Steffa is having a day in bed." The nature of Steffa's problem was never explained.

Sophie abruptly changed the subject, as she often did, sometimes leaving me panting to keep up. "Let's go to the new Bergman movie tomorrow night. Can you? Say yes."

"Yes, yes, but then I'll have to work all day Sunday."

"And after the movie there's a party in Montparnasse. We can go together."

"Oh, no, I don't think so."

"Christine, it will be fun. You're too serious all the time. You need to relax and enjoy yourself."

"I'm older than the other students. I feel out of place."

"Nonsense. The students are all ages. Come, we'll have a time, you'll see."

Sophie's energy was boundless. Somehow she managed to be a full-time student, to work, to take care of her sister, and to have fun. She loved movies and concerts and plays and parties. She loved to sit in a café and discuss the latest François Truffaut film, the new Georges Brassens record, the current production at the Comédie Française, the just published novel by André Maurois, the recent absurdity perpetrated by the government. She could discourse at length on almost any subject, even those she didn't know very much about. She had a limitless curiosity about the United States. One day she said, "Tell me everything about your time in America, I mean everything," and she did mean everything. She interrogated me unmercifully.

Sometimes Sophie made me tired with her energy and I had to take a few days off from her. But I always returned, for she added immeasurably to my life. We had connected somehow on a profound level. I think she felt this too. I could not articulate in what way we were bound together, by what intangible thread, but I knew it to be true. I could not be long without her. She was a life force that somehow infused me, hesitant and insecure, with a necessary strength.

One day she took me by surprise. "Come to my place for tea," she said. Tea! She never drank tea. Beer, coffee, wine, pastis—these were the beverages she imbibed along with her ubiquitous Gauloises cigarettes. I had never seen her take a cup of tea. And she had never invited me to her home before, though she had been to mine on several occasions.

I arrived at the appointed time. Sophie answered the door to her apartment, in a run-down building on rue de la Verrerie, and when I crossed the threshold I had to suppress a gasp, so surprised was I at the appearance of the place. A wooden table surrounded by three rickety wooden chairs, a soiled and broken sofa and armchair were the only furnishings. Against the far wall was a shelf on which rested a hot plate and a few dishes, cups, and glasses. Below the shelf was a cupboard hidden from view by a flowered curtain behind which, I presumed, were stored foodstuffs and cooking utensils. Under the window was a cot covered in a tattered cloth that did not qualify as a proper bedspread any more than the cot could be called a proper bed. I wondered if there were sheets beneath the cloth, but, more importantly, I wondered why there was only one cot for the two sisters. I had to conclude that one of them, probably Sophie, slept on the awful sofa.

I had not realized until now that I had never seen the inner realms of real poverty. And though I had never seen poverty, I recognized it immediately in the place where Sophie lived. My little apartment, with its simple yet comfortable, clean, and intact furnishings had not seemed luxurious until now. My little kitchen had seemed barely adequate until I saw the circumstances in which Sophie had to prepare her meals.

Sophie greeted me warmly and seemingly without any self-consciousness about her squalid living quarters. She introduced me to her sister, who sat curled up like a shy puppy in the battered armchair. "You are Sophie's new friend," Steffa said as she looked up at me with her black soft eyes. "I'm so happy to meet you at last," I said. Steffa did not look sickly as I had expected. She was thin, but she had a good color to her complexion, her eyes were clear, her handshake firm. There was nothing about her appearance that betrayed whatever the infirmity was from which she suffered.

Sophie made us all a cup of tea which she served with a plate of tinned biscuits. I sorely wished I had brought something with me, something special for them to eat. I had never thought to find them in such extreme circumstances. Next time, I thought, with regret.

"Steffa is thinking of taking up her studies again. I've been telling her it is never too late to learn."

"Indeed. I've just resumed my studies after three years away. I didn't like the work I'd been doing, so I'm starting over. I'm going for a history degree. I want to teach and to write a book one day. Sophie is right, I think, it is never too late." It was difficult to calculate Steffa's age, though I judged her to be quite a bit older than her sister, who, at age twenty-four, was in her last year at university.

"Steffa was preparing for a degree in physics when her studies were interrupted."

Sophie did not elaborate further, leaving me curious about what had caused the interruption. I was at a loss for words, feeling I had to be careful what I said. "That's a shame," was all I could manage.

"In the fall perhaps. We are planning on the fall semester, aren't we, Steffa?"

Steffa did not answer. "Yes, the fall, I think," Sophie answered for her. "Papa always said that education was the most important thing, for daughters as well as sons. He was adamant about that, always, his girls were to be educated the same as his boys, no difference." Sophie smiled at Steffa and patted her hand. "In the fall, perhaps. We'll see. We'll see."

Suddenly Sophie looked very sad. I wondered where the boys were to whom she referred, her brothers. I wondered if her Papa was dead. She had never spoken before of any relatives except Steffa. And I had never asked, trying, I think, to avoid any conversation about family, not wanting to talk about my own.

"I'm going for the advanced degree in history," I said, trying to defuse the melancholy air that had unaccountably descended on the three of us at the mention of Sophie and Steffa's absent family. "It will take more time, but I think it will be worth it in the end, I will have greater opportunities."

"You've decided then. Bravo, Christine. I am happy. Good decision. You'll be a great and learned historian and we shall all come to you for wisdom," Sophie exclaimed and laughed. Her sadness had lasted but a moment before her exuberance returned. For the rest of my visit Sophie talked and talked about this and that, jumping about from subject to subject, smoking her Gauloises, the way she always did.

When it came time for me to leave, I invited Sophie and Steffa to dinner three days hence. I had an overwhelming desire to feed them both a good and nourishing meal, to bestow upon them all manner of food and furniture as well as monetary assistance. Making a fine meal for them seemed the only practical possibility at the moment and I was disquieted when Sophie said, "Well, not this week, but the next time Steffa comes for a visit, well, then we should be happy to take you up on your kind invitation."

"Comes for a visit?"

"Steffa does not live here," Sophie said. "Did you think? Oh, no, this is no place for Steffa. She lives, well she lives in Montmorency actually, not far. She comes for a visit when she can manage. Like today. For a visit. And now that she is getting better and better, she will come more often, and then, when I graduate and get a good job, we shall have a place together, a fine place where we shall live in decent style, when I have a good wage. Won't we, Steffa?"

Steffa smiled at her sister. Her expression was almost one of indulgence, as though her sister's plans were flights of fancy.

Outside on the rue de la Verrerie, I stood staring down the small, winding street, weighed down by all the unanswered questions about Sophie and Steffa. The convivial feeling from my visit had vanished, and I realized that Steffa, except for a few words of greeting and farewell, had not spoken during my entire visit. Whatever her illness, it was not one of the body, I decided, but one of the spirit. I wondered if it was akin to my own.

On the way back from Le Marais where Sophie lived to my apartment near Les Invalides, I was confronted for the first time since my return to Paris with Notre Dame Cathedral. I no longer attended Sunday Mass, I no longer worshipped as I once had done, so I do not know what compelled me to enter the great basilica. In my worry about Sophie's apparent destitution and Steffa's unspecified illness, I suppose I fell back on the old habit of seeking solace from God and from the Virgin Mary. It was a mistake. As soon as I entered, as soon as I saw all the candles lit by the faithful for their intentions, I was overcome by the flickering flames that surrounded me. Fire. I could not stand the sight of fire, even in such a benign and contained form as the tiny flames of votive candles, for the images of conflagration they evoked were insupportable. Even when I lit my gas burners, when Sophie struck a match for her cigarette, I had to avert my eyes for fear that my mind would be ignited once again.

I fled the Gothic edifice. I stood on the sidewalk looking up at the two square towers and the gargoyles laughing and grimacing at the people below, and I felt unspeakably alone. It was clear to me in that moment that of all I had ever lost— my family and my childhood home, my close and innocent relationship with Mother Céline and the other nuns at the convent, the girls I had grown up with, my sisters, all scattered now—I missed God the most. He had been the support and structure of my life; now I was collapsed into myself. He had been all power, all love, all mercy; now only the power, uninvolved and cruel, remained. I had been made in His image; now I was but air and water and bone. I once believed He had died that I might live; now I knew that I and all of my kind were condemned to eternal dust. My redemption had never been achieved. Good and evil were but two sides of the same coin, alternating randomly, no greater odds for one over the other. Suffering was just pain and anguish, without grace or merit, to be avoided at all costs or endured with no accounting or earned credit.

I could not see the God I used to worship within the history to which I would dedicate my life. All I could see was firestorm—London, Dresden, Hiroshima; was Holocaust—flaming ovens, spewing chimneys, human ash. All I could see of God was His permission.

Within the unholy history, there was a tiny place called Oradour, so infinitesimal, almost invisible within the atrocious whole, my own personal burnt offering, not an incandescence but an eternal immolation. And within the infinitesimal there was the woman in my dreams, the woman in the flowered dress, holding her two little children as God allowed them to die, her agony to me far greater than any a god-man had suffered on a cross.

The god-man who was said to be human in all ways but sin was a fraud, for He was possessed of the omniscience that belongs only to an almighty being. In His death throes, despite His cry, "My God, my God, why hast Thou forsaken me?" the god-man had the comfort of a certain knowledge that His words did not fall on the deaf ears of an uninvolved deity, that He would rise again, would, within three days, enter eternal Paradise. Did the woman in the flowered dress have such certainty as she died? How would that be possible? If she did possess such a faith, I could no longer manage it.

As the nuns believe that Christ is crucified anew each day by sin, I believe that the woman in the flowered dress also dies anew each day, for I see her dying over and over, in my mind's eye, awake and asleep. Her cross is before me always, not in an abstract, symbolic way, but with the bloody, tortured body hanging from the wood.

My God, my God why hast Thou forsaken me? My whispered words hung in the air and fell to the pavement, breaking into pieces at my feet.

2

I drew my rooms tight around me. I pulled the drapes across
the French windows blocking out the rooftops cluttered
with dormers and chimney pots spread out below; the Eiffel
Tower, an iron sentinel, rising behind; the tops of the chestnut trees, just starting to bud in anticipation of spring
warmth and reaching toward the wrought-iron railing around
my little verandah. I locked the door. I took the phone off
the hook.

I drew my body tight around me. I lay beneath the quilt
that Mother Marguerite had made for me when I was a
young girl and which, having need of something tangible
from my childhood, I had taken from the convent when I left
after my last visit. I closed my eyes. I stared into the darkness within my head, and if an image formed there against
my will, I refused it, banished it from my inner eye. I
thought hard of black space, limitless, empty, and with practice and concentration I was able, for long stretches of time,
to maintain my mind in nothingness. I was unable, however,
to exclude the voices from next door, the singing that fell
upon my ears. I concentrated on the beauty of the sounds,

just the sounds, rising and falling, loud and soft, not allowing them to evoke concrete images or specific emotions that would intrude on the darkness within.

I remained so for hours, lost in black time. I gave no thought to my classes, to the editing work on the desk, the deadlines looming. I worked only to prevent thought, to abolish cognition. Occasionally, against my will, the darkness was penetrated by forms of light, but I forced them to remain abstract, arcane.

From time to time I slept and then, of course, I lost control of my inner darkness. My dreams, as though to mock my determined nothingness, depicted vividly my little town of long ago, my mother and my father going about their day unaware of the disaster to come, and me, a child, and yet grown, trying to warn them, trying to tell them to run, to hide in the forest. I have a hiding place for you, I told them, but they did not hear. I was angry, but even my anger did not reach them. Why do you not pay attention? Why don't you run, take the babies and run? But I was invisible, inaudible, and they went their eternal way to a doom they could not foresee. When I awoke, helpless, gasping with the futility of changing the course of past events, I again set about pulling darkness over the images that remained from my sleep, covering everything, by a great force of will, with blank blackness.

I would not have been able to maintain this suspended state for long. I would have run out of strength soon enough. But I was still in darkness when there came a knocking on my door, soft at first, then louder, insistent, accompanied by a familiar voice begging me to open, pleading. It was a voice

I could not refuse. I had thought I was protected from intrusion in my rooms within rooms, by the double doors, my own and then the outer door to the stair landing. Sometimes a student or the maid left the outer door ajar, as must have happened on this day, for Sophie, to whom the insistent voice belonged, had made it past the first barrier and, by the force of her knocking, was threatening to break down the second. I opened to permit my friend entrance, to prevent any damage to Monsieur Bernac's property, and to avoid any alarm on the part of my landlord that I had loud and rowdy friends. Sophie took one look at me and her face assumed a stricken expression.

"My God, what has happened to you?"

"Happened? Nothing. Nothing has happened."

Sophie pushed her way past me. "Nothing? You look like death dug up. It's the middle of the day, though you'd never know it in here, it's so dark. And you're in your nightclothes. Are you ill? Why didn't you call? Are you ill?"

"No, no, I'm fine, really."

"You don't look fine. You haven't been in class. You don't answer the phone. What has happened, Christine? Tell me at once." Sophie was used to getting her way, it seemed, to having her questions answered. "You have made me worry. I don't like to worry."

"I'm sorry."

"Say what it is, Christine, so I don't worry."

"I, I've, I am not from Fontvielle, as I told you. Well, that's not right. I am from Fontvielle, but not originally. I only came to Fontvielle when I was six years old."

"What has that got to do with anything?"

"Something happened to me in America. Something happened that made me remember things. I had a memory, a flashback I guess you could say, from my childhood, from my early childhood, before I went to live in Fontvielle. Things have not been the same for me since. I, that is, now, since I returned to France, I have confirmed that memory, the memory is real. And more. I remember more, little by little, day by day. And these new memories are real. My recurring dreams are real."

"My God, Christine, what memories? What do you remember? I don't understand what you are trying to tell me."

"I was born and lived until I was six years old in a small town called Oradour-sur-Glane. Do you see? Do you see what I am saying? I am from Oradour."

Sophie squinted her eyes as though someone had shone a light in her face. Her mouth tightened. Her hand came up from her side, the palm outward as though she were warding off a blow. She understood. She had not said a word, but I could see she understood. She knew what had happened. She saw what I was saying. As others recognize the words Auschwitz and Hiroshima and Dresden and Lidice, Sophie recognized the word Oradour and she knew what it meant.

"Oh my dear, sweet friend. How brave you are. How you have suffered and how very brave you are," Sophie said, and she took me in her arms.

America, 1963

3

"Christine, this is Howie Black, Jim Epley and Brian Malloy. All *World* writers, I'm bound to say, so you'll have to put up with them. Howie is International, Jim, National, and Brian, our expert in making the arcane intelligible, is Science and Medicine. Gentlemen, meet Christine Lenoir of our Paris office."

"Christine. A pleasure. How generous of our Paris office. Welcome to New York."

"Very pleased to meet you, Christine. From Paris! Christine Lenoir, is it? Yes? I second that. Welcome, indeed. New York can always use another pretty girl, especially a French girl, other than there are none prettier, in my humble opinion."

I couldn't catch that last part, right after "especially a French girl." The rest of the sentence didn't make any sense to me, probably some slang with which I wasn't familiar. American men often behaved in a foolish manner on meeting me, on finding out I am French. I had come to the conclusion, in the short time I had been in New York, that American males thought of all French females as a great sexual opportunity, willing and adept, definitely adept. It was, I

33

think, the intimate tone they used to say my name or to comment on my nationality that somehow always seemed inappropriate. It was the way they shook my hand, holding on just a little longer than was seemly. It was the things they said, like "How generous of our Paris office," or "New York can always use another pretty girl," in a low voice that had a slightly salacious quality. Their attitude toward me was never businesslike, always had a personal edge that was very unnerving.

The third gentlemen just introduced to me didn't say anything. He looked at me with a shy smile and bowed his head slightly.

The maître d' acknowledged by name the man who had just made all the introductions. "Bonjour, Monsieur Jacobson. How nice to see you. Your table is ready." His French accent seemed genuine, perhaps a good sign for the meal to come.

We followed the maître d' to a corner table dressed in starched white linen and adorned with fresh flowers, gold-rimmed plates and wine goblets. Extravagant bouquets were everywhere about the room and all the tables were occupied by talking, gesturing, laughing people drinking martinis and whiskey and working hard to impress one another. Business expense accounts definitely made this little world go round, and I suspected that the ambiance was better than the food. So far I had been unimpressed with the New York restaurants, costly all, where I had been wined and dined since my arrival. Of course, I never had to pay for these meals, but I had to appear enthusiastic, eating more than I wanted, drinking more than was my custom. I always felt that my table companions were waiting for my approval of the meal as though all French people were gourmets. And the man who chose the wine always seemed to deliberate a bit longer than necessary, eyeing me warily over the top of the wine list, probably assuming that all French, even females, are experts on the subject and that I was watching him for any misstep or gaucherie.

Actually, my preference in food runs to the simple provincial fare on which I had been raised rather than meals served in Michelin three-star restaurants. And my knowledge of wine is pretty much restricted to those made from the vineyards near my home. Of course, never wanting to disappoint, I always feigned enthusiasm about the elaborate and saucy dishes that had been set before me since my arrival in America, and I always praised the over-priced wine. I tried to finish most of the food on my plate, even though the portions were too large and making conversation with strangers in English while eating at the same time was always difficult for me. I speak very good English, having studied the language from an early age, but the local argot sometimes was elusive, especially over the din of a crowded restaurant. In any case, I had already learned to order small, to choose a fish meunière, which was the offering most likely to be simple and easy to eat while I concentrated on the conversation.

"Well, Christine Lenoir of Paris, France, when did you arrive in New York?" Jim Epley asked.

"I have been here about a month, since the beginning of September."

"Are you enjoying our fair city?" Howie Black inquired.

"New York is a big and exciting place. I must try not to be overwhelmed."

"Well, now you know three coworkers willing to give you a hand whenever you feel overwhelmed, doesn't she, gentlemen?" Mark Jacobson said this with a sweeping gesture of his arm that almost overturned a wine goblet.

"Yes, well, that is very nice, thank you."

"Don't you just love the way she talks?" Jim Epley said to no one in particular. "I just love the way she talks." Then he turned directly to me. "I just love the way you talk. Talk to me some more, Christine Lenoir of Paris, France. Or better yet, say something to us in French. I bet I can understand. Go on, say something. Just don't make it too hard."

I felt like a performing seal. I squinted my eyes and pursed my lips against my distress and embarrassment. I looked across the table at Brian Malloy, who so far had said not one single word, and he shook his head and rolled his eyes slightly in acknowledgment of my discomfort. "Why don't we all stick to English, Jim," he said. "With your pitiful high school French you might not know when she is insulting you."

"Christine wouldn't do that, would you Christine?"

"Why don't we order," Brian said, rescuing me again. "I have a busy afternoon."

"Hey, what about some drinks?" Jim said.

"In honor of Christine, how about some French wine instead," Mark Jacobson said and he signaled for the waiter. He read the wine list with a look of insecurity that I felt was uncharacteristic for a senior editor of *World* magazine. I tried not to look at him, but when he finally ordered, a 1961 Pouilly Fuissé, his eyes settled on me for just a moment, but that was long enough for me to notice the need for my approval. I smiled, not having the slightest idea how good a choice he had made, and he looked pleased. When the wine had been tasted, approved, and poured, Mark Jacobson raised his glass. "Welcome to Christine. We all look forward to getting to know her and to working with her."

The four men raised their wine glasses and drank. I squirmed in my seat and concentrated on the condensation making little rivulets down the slopes of the plain, tall goblets.

"Aren't you drinking?" Jim Epley said almost accusingly. Having been taught that it is improper to drink a toast to oneself, I was confused by his question. But I picked up my glass and took a sip of the cold, smooth liquid. Jim Epley looked satisfied. "Very nice," I said, even though the wine tasted quite ordinary to me, and Mark Jacobson looked proud as a peacock.

"Christine is here for a year or so as part of a new company policy, a sort of a foreign exchange program if you will, so that our writers can experience different parts of the world, expand their horizons," Mark Jacobson said. "Jason McPherson has gone to Paris to write about Europe from the perspective of an American, and Christine is here to give us her unique view of America from the perspective of a French woman, a European. We feel that everyone will benefit—the writers, the magazine, our readers."

The conversation then turned away from me, for which I was very grateful, and to stories that were in the planning stage. I hated talking about business over food, but it was better than talking about myself.

The salad was served, the plate crowded with greens drenched in vinaigrette. Even in restaurants pretending to be

French, the salad came before the entrée, which seemed to rather spoil the appetite instead of acting as an aid to digestion as the small, delicate salads served after an authentic French meal are intended to do. At least the lettuce was not topped off with grated carrots or red onions or, dear heaven, cubes of bread or bacon bits or chunks of cheese as they often are in American eateries. Still, all I could manage were a few bites, reserving my energies for what was to come. No one seemed to notice my lack of enthusiasm as the men ate with gusto, talking all the while.

Later, as I stood on the sidewalk outside the restaurant surrounded by men fueled by their lunch and behaving with bravado, as though ready to take on the world, I wondered how I would find the energy to get through the afternoon.

"Well, it was a great pleasure. I'm off to an interview uptown. We'll do it again soon, yes, indeed. I look forward to working with you, Christine Lenoir of Paris, France."

I looked at Brian and he was laughing soundlessly. "Thank you very much, Jim Epley of New York City, United States of America." Now Brian was laughing right out loud. The sound was infectious and I laughed too, releasing the tension that had built up inside me during the endless meal.

Brian walked at my side back to the *World* office building. Mark Jacobson and Howie Black wended their way ahead of us, navigating with expertise the lunchtime crowds.

"I usually hate these lunches," Brian said. "Food and business just don't go together. Not good for the digestion.

And then I end up half asleep for the better part of the afternoon. But I must confess, today's lunch was rather entertaining in its way. I think you might agree. Grown men can be pretty silly sometimes. And I got to meet you, after all." If Jim Epley had said this last, it would have sounded like a come-on. But the words as they came from Brian Malloy were matter-of-fact, easy, and seemed without innuendo. We reached the lobby of the *World* headquarters and Brian said, "I'll leave you here. I'm off myself, for a meeting with a mad scientist at Columbia. See ya soon, Christine Lenoir, of Paris, France."

He said this last in a mimicking, mocking way that I'm certain Jim Epley, writer for the Nation section of *World* magazine, would not have appreciated. I liked the man of Science and Medicine. He made me laugh, something I had not done a lot since coming to America.

4

It felt as though all the oxygen had been sucked out of the room by a firestorm and I waited with trepidation for the vacuum to be filled. But nothing happened. Everyone just sat in silence and waited. The man at the head of the long table was reading from typed pages in front of him. He seemed oblivious to the other people seated around the table. There was no talking, no whispering among the expectant underlings. Not even a cough or a sneeze. I felt an inexplicable urge to clear my throat, but I didn't dare so I just swallowed hard. It was clear that whatever would eventually fill the empty space around us would have to come from the short, broad, middle-aged, balding man, for he held all the power. I was glad I was seated far away from him, between Jim Epley and Julia Richardson, the picture editor, for I actually felt afraid of the managing editor of *World* magazine. And fear, while an emotion I had not often experienced, seemed, in this moment, a familiar sensation.

Brian Malloy wasn't in attendance at this weekly editorial meeting I had been told was mandatory. I made a mental note to ask him how he had managed to be absent, hoping for a means of escape for myself in the future. Assuming, of course, that Mr. Malloy was still employed after today's truancy.

"The Kennedys! I'm sick to death of them! I know a Kennedy cover sells, but for Christ's sake, enough is enough!" Anatole Osterwald had spoken at last, and it wasn't a pleasant sound. His words, controlled but angry, rasped through the air and reached my ears encased in a German accent which I had not anticipated, and my fear exploded within me. He looked out from under bushy eyebrows, through deep, black eyes and he scowled. "And Julia, I don't like the cover picture. Get me another one, something with a serious expression. I'm sick to death of looking at Kennedy teeth."

The picture editor got up from her chair next to mine and left the room without saying one single word. I felt exposed and vulnerable on my right flank by her departure.

"Marty, what's this upcoming story on Vietnam? I need to know about this. This is a goddamn touchy issue right now. Who the hell is reporting on this? I don't recognize all these names I see here on the story list. I need to be goddamn sure that a story on Vietnam is well researched, that those reporters know what the hell they're doing. You understand?"

I expected Marty Gershon to at least say that he understood, but he remained silent. Mr. Osterwald didn't seem to expect a response, he just forged ahead with his questions, which were always more accusations than inquiries; with his comments, which were always criticism, full of crude language and epithets, and never expressions of pleasure or approval. In every sentence he seemed to take the Lord's name in vain, something which I still believed was a sin and which deeply offended me. As the man with the German accent continued his tirade, breaking the first commandment over and over, I wondered if there was anything about the magazine or the people working for it that he liked, for displeasure was the only aspect of the role he was playing, irritation and disdain were the only attributes of his one-dimensional performance.

He went down the story list for the next four weeks, questioning the editor or writer in charge of one story or another. "Jim, for Christ's sake, this is an original idea," Anatole Osterwald said sarcastically to the man on my left. If Jim Epley got up to fetch something for the head man, I would be left totally unprotected. I decided I would have to go with him. "Jesus Christ, how many stories have we done lately on Martin Luther King? I'm sick of the Kennedys and I'm sick of this Negro and his marches. You're getting lazy, Mr. Epley. I want to see you earn your money. A topic we haven't done fifty times already would be nice."

Jim Epley leaned over and whispered in my ear, "The man is a fascist pig, Christine," the first words spoken by anyone other than the tyrant at the head of the long, shiny table. I thought I might have to change my mind about Jim Epley. Yes, I might have to revise my thinking. Maybe the man wasn't silly after all.

"Well, Jesus, that's all I can take of this shit for the time being. Get the hell out of here, all of you, and do some god-damn work for a change." I half expected the man to shout "alle raus."

Everyone started to rise. "Wait a minute, wait just a little minute." Mr. Osterwald leaned toward the man on his right and said, "Who is this?" pointing to the story list. "I don't recognize this name. Is this someone new since I've been gone? Christ, I take a little vacation and everything falls apart, new people are brought in and I'm never even told about it. Christine Lenoir? Are you here? Speak up. Is she here, for Christ's sake?"

"Yes, sir, I'm here," I said, raising my hand like a stupid schoolgirl.

"Well, yes, there you are. And where did you come from, if I may ask?"

"I am from the Paris bureau. The exchange program. I am here for a year, while Jason McPherson is in Paris."

"Oh, yes, Steven Hollander's idiotic idea, an exchange program, like we're running a goddamn Fulbright instead of a news magazine. Where are you from?"

"I'm, well, I'm from Paris, sir."

"Yes, yes, the Paris bureau, you said. But where are you from, born, where do you come from originally, what city or town?"

"Oh, I see, I'm from, well, I'm from a town near Aix-en-Provence, in the south. . . ."

"Yes, yes, I know Aix-en-Provence. Been there many times. My wife is from France, too, you know."

Mr. Osterwald had asked what town I was from, but he hadn't waited for my answer. I could see he was a man who didn't really listen to others, who didn't put much stock in what anyone other than himself had to say. He had probably heard Aix-en-Provence and had simply decided that that answer was close enough. "Yes, sir, well, no," I stammered, "That is, no, I didn't know that your wife is French."

"From Strasbourg. That's where we met. In Alsace."

"Yes, sir, I know. It is a lovely city."

"Yes, it is. Well, Mademoiselle Lenoir, it is Mademoiselle?"

"Yes, it is."

"Well, Mademoiselle Lenoir, or should I call you Ms. Lenoir now that you're here in the land of the goddamn feminists, I hope you profit from your time with us. Christine Lenoir. Nice name. Looks good on a page. Maybe you can teach these idiots working here something useful, as long as we're now running a goddamn Fulbright program. Never approved of the idea, but who knows, maybe something good will come of it. Your story is on childcare this week? Soft, Christine, very soft. Take on something harder next time, something with an edge. Hard. Do something hard. Make us blink."

I didn't have any idea what the man with the horrible German accent and the nasty disposition and the blasphemous mouth was talking about. I couldn't imagine a topic more important, harder if you will, than the welfare of a nation's children. And frankly, if I had but had the nerve, I would have told the arrogant fascist pig facing me across the expanse of table that American society was doing a goddamn, may the Lord forgive me, poor job providing for its young. Blink, blink, blink.

5

Jim Epley stopped in my doorway. "Hey, Christine, we're going down to Tung Hoy for a few pops. Wanna come?"

A few pops. I was certainly bewildered the first time I heard that expression. "No, thanks, Jim. I'm tired. Think I'll just go on home."

"It's Friday. You can't just go home. You can sleep all day tomorrow. Just for a little while. One drink. Come on, Christine. It'll do you good."

"Okay. One. I mean it, just one."

"One it is. And it's on me."

The bar at the Chinese restaurant two doors down from the *World* office building was jammed with Friday afternoon revelers having more than just a few pops. Jim and I squeezed our way toward the editorial contingent from *World* in their usual place at the far end of the long bar. Everyone had started early this week because the magazine had closed on time, a somewhat rare occurrence. I had been introduced to this Friday ritual my very first week, and it was not my idea of a good time. I hated people pushing and shoving me, and the noise of the place made it hard for me to follow the conversation.

"What'll it be, Christine?" Jim asked.

"Please, a glass of white wine."

"You haven't taken to our whiskey yet? Try one, for a change."

"No, please. No whiskey. A sherry, dry, is also fine. If they have."

"They have anything your little heart desires."

"Sherry, then, please."

"Sherry it is. Dry."

"Hi, there, Christine. Over here. How are you? This is terrible, isn't it. Why don't all these people go home to their families? How are you?"

It was Brian Malloy of Science and Medicine. I was grateful for the sight of him. "I'm fine, fine, thank you."

"Well, you look fine, I must say. Haven't seen you since that lunch, Christine Lenoir of Paris, France. When was that? Must be two weeks ago now. Glad to see you haven't been completely overwhelmed by New York or *World*. Hey Jim, how's it going?"

Jim handed me a sherry and leaned his body into mine. He put his arm across my shoulders. I tried to squirm away, but there was no room to move. I don't like being touched by people I hardly know. It makes me very uncomfortable. But I was trapped.

"Not bad. All things considered. You?"

"Hangin' in. Just telling Christine that I haven't laid eyes on her since lunch that day. Been out of town on a story."

"Well, she just survived her first encounter with our great leader. He was his usual, you know. You can't let Osterwald get to you, Christine. You'd think he was a Storm Trooper if you didn't know he was a German Jew who had to run when the Nazis took over. How lucky we were that he ended up here. Anyway, you get used to him. All managing editors are bastards. It's a prerequisite for the job. I understand that Robards, the M.E. at *World Sports*, makes the women cry and the men toss their cookies on quite a regular basis."

Toss their cookies? Is that what he said? Before I had a chance to ask, Brian said, "Well, I, for one, don't believe it's necessary to be cruel in order to produce a good magazine. Just because Osterwald is a German Jew who had to flee the Nazis doesn't make him a decent person. He's a prick as far as I'm concerned." I knew that one already, prick, had heard it quite a few times as a matter of fact. Another staff writer, thankfully a woman, had told me what the slang word meant. "And he's also a bigot who often lets his prejudices and his personal politics into his editorial policy."

"My, my, Brian, harsh words. At the story meeting this morning he told Christine to make us blink. Blink, mind you. He's such an asshole. Don't pay him any mind, Christine. Most of it is just an act. Anyway, you've got me blinking already."

Jim Epley leaned in close to my face and blinked his eyes at me. I tried to back away but I was hemmed in on all sides. I felt a hand close around mine. I thought it must be Jim's hand, but before I could make a fuss, I was being pulled through the crowd. I could see then that it was Brian Malloy who had possession of my hand and the rest of me as well.

47

"Hey, wait a minute," I heard Jim Epley call above the din. "Just wait a goddamn minute. Malloy, what the hell do you think you're doing?"

"Just need a little breathing room, Jim," Brian called back to his coworker, but I'm sure Jim couldn't hear him above the noise. "There, that's better," he said as he maneuvered me into a little space by the front window. "Sorry, didn't mean to act like Tarzan, but I could see Jim making the move on you and you were uncomfortable."

"Move on me?"

"Ummm, a little too much touching and feeling, more than you wanted I think."

"More than I wanted."

"Another drink?"

"No, no, I don't think so."

"Would you like to get out of here?"

"Yes, I would. Very much."

"Good. How about some dinner? Someplace quiet."

"Is there any place in New York that is quiet on a Friday evening?"

"You just leave that up to me."

"It's not very fancy and it'll get noisy later on, but for now we can have a little peace."

"How did you manage to get this nice corner booth? I don't see many empty tables and it's just the two of us."

"Pull."

"Pull?"

"Pull, uhhh, influence. I play rugby in my spare time, and this is a rugby hangout. In here a lot, I'm ashamed to say. The place is owned by a couple of old rugby guys I happen to know and they always treat the players well."

"I thought rugby was a European game."

"It is, really. Most of the guys I play with are displaced persons from Ireland and England and Australia. I played football in college. Was never good enough for the pros but hated to give it up. Rugby is the closest I could come."

"It's pretty dangerous, isn't it?"

"Not dangerous really, but rough. Keeps me off the streets and in the emergency room. Kinda stupid, huh? But guys are stupid. Jocks are anyway."

"Jocks?"

"Athletes. Guys who spend too much time playing sports, watching sports, or talking about sports. Jocks. Silly word, isn't it. Slang must drive you nuts."

"Sometimes, yes. One good thing. Once you get a slang word you never forget it. Now I think I shall always know what jock means."

"If that does you any good."

"You never know when a word will come in handy."

"Now the food here isn't anything great. Just old American hamburgers and fries, chili, that sort of thing."

"Well, that's why I'm here, to learn about American life and culture."

"Just look around you, American culture at its finest."

"I like hamburgers. It's so funny the way Americans think of the French, that all of us are gourmets and wine connoisseurs."

"Well, aren't you?"

"Actually, my taste in food and wine is really quite simple."

"Well, that's very interesting. A woman after my own heart."

"After my own heart?"

"Let's see, a woman with whom I have something in common, in this case, simple tastes. Speaking of simple, I'm going to have a beer. A glass of wine for you? Don't expect too much from the wine in this place."

"I'll have a beer too. An American beer."

"Don't carry this American culture thing too far. You don't have to have an American beer."

"I want one. A Budweiser, please."

"Budweiser it is. Hey, Kevin, two Buds, please. Now, Christine, tell me, how are you doing at old *World* magazine? I mean, how are you really doing? Every time I see you, well, you don't look real happy."

"Oh, dear, how awful. Do I walk around looking like I'm miserable?"

"Well, I don't see you very often, but at lunch that day, and tonight at Hoy's . . . "

"I'm homesick. That's mostly what it is. I'm still adjusting."

"Never been to the United States before?"

"Never."

"It must be hard. I'm sure we take a lot of getting used to. Don't ever tell anyone, but I was homesick when I first went away to college. I come from a small town in Massachusetts and when I got to this fancy college in New Jersey I felt really lost. I thought everyone was going to be rich and snobby and intellectual and I would be really out of place. But you know what, they weren't at all. I made some really great friends, guys I'm still very tight with today."

"Tight?"

"I've got to watch that. I never realized that I converse totally in slang. Tight with, let's see, close to, good friends with. That's all you need, a few good friends. I bet you'll find most people are nice enough when you get to know them. Even Epley. He means well, he just loves the girls and can't keep his hands or his enthusiasm to himself. You haven't been here long enough. Give us a chance, you'll see."

"I'm already seeing, thanks to you. Which college?"

"Oh, Princeton."

"That's very famous. Princeton. I know of it."

"Yes, I suppose it is. Joy filled our house, I can tell you, when I got in, my parents were so proud. I was too, truth be told. Anyway, it was a great four years. I miss it."

"What did you study? Journalism?"

"No, actually, I majored in biology. Always loved science. Since I was a kid rummaging around the salt marshes looking for flora and fauna. Might have been a juvenile delinquent, but I didn't have time. Every second I wasn't in school or playing football, I was watching the plants and animals. Just off the coast where I come from are breeding grounds of the humpback whales. My dad used to take me out in his boat in the fall when they migrate, and Christine, you've never seen anything like it, those whales. It's really something to watch. You should see them sometime. Anyway, I majored in biology. Then went on to Columbia for my master's."

"How did you end up at *World*?"

"I was tired of being poor. I had loans from grad school. My parents had paid out a fortune for Princeton, I couldn't ask them to pay more. Wanted to get out of debt, so it was money. I sold my soul for the money. But I've been at the magazine for three years now, plenty long enough to know that I'm in the wrong place. I don't like the editorial policy, I don't respect Osterwald. But it's more than that. I don't like bringing everything down to the common denominator, I mean, simplifying everything so it fits into the small space *World* magazine is willing to give to science and medicine and technology."

"There are science magazines."

"Yes, I've thought of it. But what I really want to do is go back and get my Ph.D. and teach. I think I would make a good teacher and science needs good teachers, teachers who love it and can make their students love it too. This country is going to need more scientists in the future and we'd better have some good, creative teachers."

"Well, then?. . . "

"My loans are all paid off now, and I'm trying to save enough to do it. Takes money, Christine."

"Well, I hope you do it. Being a teacher, well that is a wonderful thing. Helping young people."

"What about you? How did you end up at *World*?"

"I was given the gift of a very fine education, as you were. Although I'm lucky, I have no loans. My education was for free. When I finished university, I had never been anywhere really. I had never seen anything of the world. I had been quite, well, I don't know the word. . . ."

"Sheltered?"

"Yes, maybe, sheltered. I had no experience of the world. Is that what sheltered means?"

"Exactly."

"And my, well, my family thought I should have some experience before I made a final decision about what I wanted to do. I heard about this job, and since I speak English. . . ."

"How is that you speak English so well?"

"I had the finest education. I had English lessons from the time I was six years old."

"Six years old!"

"Europeans believe it is important to learn languages and that you must start early. Children learn languages very easily, naturally. When you are in your adolescence, it is already more difficult. In my family English was often spoken, and I had English classes as soon as I started school. Anyway, I applied for the job at the Paris bureau and I got it. It was nice working there. A small bureau where everyone knew everyone else, everyone helped everyone else. And I had the opportunity to travel—all over—Europe, England. It was wonderful for me. Then this opportunity to come to America. I was afraid at first. I didn't want to go so far, to some place where I didn't know anyone. Actually, I'm still afraid. But my mother, that is to say, my family, thought it was a wonderful opportunity for me, and so you see, here I am, learning American slang."

"Eating American food and drinking American beer."

"And talking to a very nice American man."

"Why, thank you, Christine. I think you're already looking happier, if I may say so."

"I'm feeling happier."

"Happy and hungry, I hope."

"Very."

"Let's order. What'll it be?"

"Hamburger, of course. And fries."

"A salad?"

"Actually, I'll not have a salad. That's the one thing I'm a French snob about, salad. American salads are always too big, with too many things in it, I think. I'm not used to that."

"That's us Americans alright. The bigger, the better, the more stuff, the better we like it. Unfortunately, bigger is not always better. Hey, Kev, two hamburgers. Medium okay, Christine?"

"Yes. Okay."

"Two hamburgers, medium, tomatoes on the side, two fries, two more Buds. Thanks."

"I think you are a man after my own heart."

"I think I am too."

"I mean we have something in common. I don't think the magazine business is what I want to do either."

"What then?"

"I studied history at university."

"Where was that? The university."

"In Paris. The Sorbonne."

"Wow, like Princeton. Famous."

"Yes, just so. Well I studied history and I think I want to return to that."

"History, big field."

"Yes. I'd have to choose an area of concentration, perhaps France between the wars. I'm not certain."

"To what end? To be a teacher?"

"Perhaps, yes. A writer. I thought that was what I wanted before I went to *World*. And now I am decided. I think we must learn from history, especially recent history. We need to understand why events happened as they did, why our century has been so full of war and bloodshed."

"Well, two people with so much in common. We both know what we want, we just have to figure out how to get there."

"God will show us."

"Yes, well, never looked at it that way. But who knows, maybe God will show us. And you know what, I think our time at the magazine has not been a waste. We know more about the world, more about people. We've had time to find out what we really want and what we don't want. And I think we've both made a real good friend."

"I think so."

"How about going to my rugby match next weekend?"

"If you promise not to end up in the emergency room."

"That's a promise."

"Miss Lenoir?"

"Yes."

"You may go in now, the second cubicle on the left."

"Is he alright?"

"He's got an aching head but he'll be fine. He will be here 'til morning, just as a precaution. He's been asking for you, so go on in to see him before he goes upstairs."

"Thank you, Doctor."

I found Brian with a big bandage on his forehead and looking very contrite. "You broke your promise. You said no emergency rooms and look where we are," I said, not letting him off the hook.

"I am so sorry, Christine."

"How do you feel?"

"Stupid. A stupid jock."

"Jock! I'll certainly never forget that word now. Look at your poor head."

"Fourteen stitches. Did you know that people bleed a lot from their head? I never knew that."

"I know it now."

"God, I'm sorry. What a miserable day for you."

"You scared me half to death. Don't you ever do that again."

"I may have to retire from sports."

"I should think so. No helmets. At least football players wear helmets."

"I know, I know. It's tennis and golf from now on. Please, let me make it up to you."

"Brian, it doesn't matter as long as you're alright. You have to stay the night."

"I know. Please, take a taxi home. I'll pay for it."

"I think I can afford a taxi. I'll come pick you up in the morning and see you home."

"I don't want to cause you more trouble."

"I'll be here in the morning. I'll go to church early and then I'll come right over. I should be here by ten o'clock or so."

"That's very sweet of you, Christine."

"I cannot believe grown men play such a terrible sport."

"Me either."

"We're going to take him upstairs now," the nurse said, pushing the curtains aside. "You can go up with him if you want."

"I think I'll go home, Brian, so you can rest. See you in the morning."

"I owe you a nice dinner."

"You certainly do."

"It's a date. It'll have to be a real expensive restaurant to make this up to you."

6

"Oh, no. My God. Oh, no. Oh, my God."

The words were coming from the office next to mine. The female voice was not loud, but it was full of distress. I got up from my desk and walked toward the sounds, wondering if the woman needed help.

I had come to *World's* Miami bureau with another writer from New York to do a story on the Cuban immigrant population of this south Florida city, by all accounts an industrious and cohesive and accomplished group that had fled the Castro regime and was making a new and vibrant life in the United States. I had been given the assignment because of my Spanish, which, while not as good as my English, was still adequate, and because the editors in New York had, by now, accepted my ability.

I had just eaten a sandwich at my desk instead of going to a restaurant. I had plans to go to Key West for the weekend, and I wanted to get all my notes organized so that I could finish my report by the middle of the next week.

As I walked to the door of the office I had been given the use of for my brief stay, the distressed voice went silent.

"Jesus, he's been shot. He has. He's been shot. Son of a bitch." This was a resonant male voice, but I thought I must not have heard correctly. Someone had been shot? Some man had been shot? Is that what he had said?

I stepped out of my office into the central room where the secretaries had their desks. Everyone was wearing a bewildered expression and looking all about as though the man who had been shot was somewhere among them. Then we all gravitated to the corner office of *World*'s Miami bureau chief, Ed Feingold, where there was a television set. Ed was standing, his shirt-sleeved arms folded across his chest, looking at the black-and-white images on the screen and shaking his head.

"God Almighty, someone's shot the president," he said in a soft, calm voice. "Some fucker has just shot the president." He leaned over and changed the channel as though he hoped that someone at a different network would contradict what he had just said, would tell us that no, of course the president had not been shot, it was just a cruel hoax, a stupid mistake. Surely, some knowledgeable, informed, reliable newscaster like Chet Huntley or Walter Cronkite would appear on the screen to tell us that this terrible event had not happened, that no one had shot John F. Kennedy, the young, charismatic president of the United States of America, because, after all, who would want to do such a thing?

I had seen President Kennedy once, in 1961, shortly after I had gone to work for *World*'s Paris bureau. I had been privileged to attend a luncheon for the press during his state visit to France. His warmth, his humor, his intelligence had been very evident on that day when he introduced himself to us as the man who accompanied Jacqueline Kennedy to Paris. I had fallen completely under the spell of the charismatic American leader, as had most of my countrymen, and it now seemed inconceivable that this man of such force and such promise could be so easily eliminated from the world scene.

Ed continued around the channels, stopping a moment at each one as though searching for the words we all wanted to hear, that the president was perfectly fine. The programming on some of the channels was the usual weekday afternoon fare, game shows and soap operas, and this was reassuring, this raised hopes. Surely if the game shows and the soap operas were going on as always, everything was right with the world. But then came the bitter confirmation from the major networks. Newsmen of stature, of reliability, the Huntleys and the Brinkleys, the Cronkites and the Pettits, were all telling us, with horrific unanimity, that the president had indeed been shot at about 12:30 central standard time as he rode in a motorcade with his wife through the streets of downtown Dallas. I heard words like Dealey Plaza and Texas School Book Depository, words that had no meaning at first but which I would hear over and over during the next few days until they were indelibly and permanently etched into my brain. I had been so engrossed in my story about the Cuban immigrants, I hadn't even realized that Kennedy was going to Texas that day.

No one left Ed Feingold's office. We all waited for further information, but the same words were being repeated over and over again, adding no new information. I felt very calm. Kennedy had been shot, but I did not consider the possibility that he had been killed. It was as though I thought of him as an invincible man, some super human who could be felled but not destroyed, wounded but never killed. It was unthinkable that Kennedy was dead, and so I did not think it. I simply waited with my colleagues to learn the extent of his injuries and when he would be up and about again, leading the country, leading the non-communist world, keeping us, Americans and Europeans alike, secure and prosperous and, above all, free. And when he appeared, with a small injury, a scratch, a flesh wound, sporting a bandage, or maybe a sling, he would make us proud and, I was certain, he would make us laugh at how worried we had all been.

Then the terrible news was reported that the president had been shot in the head. Bad, I thought, this could be bad. Surgery, probably major surgery would be necessary, but he would have the best surgeon in the world and, after a few weeks in the hospital, a short convalescence in Palm Beach, he'd be right as rain.

I sat on the couch in Ed Feingold's office and waited for the confirmation that I knew would be forthcoming about Kennedy's survival. People came and went, came and went, but I paid them no mind. Ed Feingold was making one phone call after another, but I did not take in anything of what he said. It did not occur to me that I should become a participant in this drama. I saw myself only as a passive observer. No one gave me anything to do and so I did nothing but wait.

A man I did not recognize, a White House official with a grim expression, came on the television screen, and he was standing in front of the Parkland Hospital where Kennedy had been taken. "Oh God, this is it," someone in the office said. The man on the TV screen announced to the reporters and to the world that John F. Kennedy, President of the United States, was dead. Strong and vibrant, intelligent and funny, charismatic and powerful as he had been, he was dead all the same.

Pandemonium erupted in Ed Feingold's office which lasted only long enough for the bureau chief to collect himself and to call us all to order. All other stories were, of course, put on hold. Everyone would be working on the Kennedy assassination until further notice.

Since Marco Felize and I had been working on a story in the Cuban community, we were assigned to cover the reaction among these people the president had especially befriended. Kennedy and his anti-Castro stance had been very popular among those who had fled Cuba, and it was expected that there would be an intense outpouring of grief by the immigrants who had found welcome in America.

There was no time for personal pain. We worked through Friday night, into Saturday, interviewing Cuban exiles from every strata of their particular society, attending a memorial Mass in a Cuban parish, going to Cuban stores and restaurants, wandering the streets of the Cuban neighborhoods to get a feeling for the atmosphere in response to the tragedy.

Then it was back to the office to file our reports to New York. There was only one teletype machine, which was in constant demand, and the three secretaries had all they could do to keep up with the volume of material. I translated my notes and my tape recordings into more polished and organized reports and added them to the pile waiting to be teletyped by the exhausted secretaries.

By late Saturday afternoon there was a terrible lull. It seemed there was nothing more to be said, nothing more to be reported, at least for the moment. Marco and I went for dinner in a Cuban restaurant which had been full to capacity the night before, but now was almost empty. It seemed that exhaustion had set in at last, and people who had congregated together for comfort and support were now retreating within their homes, within themselves, to deal in private with the incomprehensible.

Later, in my hotel room, I telephoned Brian Malloy in New York. I wanted to know what was going on where he was.

"It's like an A-bomb went off here, like a national disaster," Brian said.

"I guess it is a national disaster."

"Are you coming back to New York?"

"I've been told to stay here, to cover the Cubans for the weekend, through the funeral on Monday. I imagine I will come back Tuesday or Wednesday, but I'm not sure. The other story I was working on has, of course, been postponed. It would be a whole different story now anyway."

"Everything will be a whole different story now."

"What's going on there?"

"Quiet. Eerie. There was a lot of activity at first, but now everything seems to have stopped. There is little traffic, very few people on the streets. I walked down to Times Square and it was empty, all the display signs were dark. The city is very strange, quiet."

"The same here. Everyone was out on the streets, in the public places. Now everyone has gone home, to grieve alone with their families, I suppose, to watch the television."

"I can't turn the television off. Even when I'm trying to get a few hours sleep. It's like a connection with everyone else, and I don't want to be alone. I wish you were here, Christine, we could have a drink and commiserate."

"Misery loves company, a good old American expression. What have you been working on?"

"Well, I'm sort of out of the mainstream type of reporting. But they've had me doing a lot of what everyone else has been doing, public reaction, memorial services. I've done a couple of interviews with some eminent scientists about what they think Kennedy's contribution was in this area. Sort of thin, but interesting, at least to me. Don't think it'll make the magazine. Well, one interview with a guy from NASA might. I got a good quote there, about the space race. Christine . . . "

"Yes?"

"Are you alright? I know how much you liked him."

"I've been so busy I haven't had time to think too much. It hasn't sunk in yet. I don't think I actually believe he's dead."

"Can you get some sleep now? You must be exhausted."

"I don't think I've ever been this tired in my life. I'm about to take a shower and go to bed."

"I'll try to be in touch tomorrow. If you don't hear from me it just means I couldn't get through. The circuits all over the country have been overloaded all day, sometimes you can't even get a dial tone. Goodnight, Christine. Sleep well."

As I got into bed, I felt apprehensive that something would happen while I slept and that I would miss it. Then I thought, how silly, the big event has already happened, the rest is just aftermath. The funeral was still more than a day away, and I couldn't imagine anything monumental occurring during the night. Yet it was funny, I still felt apprehensive as I turned off the television. Brian had said it himself, without the TV I felt all alone with the event, as though I had lost connection with the rest of the grieving world.

I was afraid I wouldn't be able to sleep, but I was so exhausted I slept well and long. I have an inner alarm clock that never fails me but, to my surprise, I overslept the next morning. Luckily, there was no demand of my presence anywhere, at least for the moment.

My first act of the new day was to turn on the television, to reconnect myself with the country and the world that was trying to adjust to what had happened, as I was trying to adjust. In my anxiety and grief, I needed the world's company. The image on the screen confirmed the new reality— the flag-draped coffin of the president on a bier in the East Room of the White House, the military guard, each from a different branch of the service, the two priests kneeling by the coffin in silent prayer, the mahogany crucifix at the foot of the coffin, the arrangement of carnations and lilies at the head, the tall candles at each corner of the bier. The funeral rites for the American president had begun.

I ordered breakfast from room service and ate staring at the coffin and the White House staff members filing silently past. I was told that tributes were pouring in from around the world. I was told that many of the world's leaders would be attending the funeral, including the head of my own country. I was told in detail the arrangements for the funeral that had been made for the most part by Mrs. Kennedy herself. I could see her as she had been in Paris during the state visit, so beautiful in her French couture. Then I saw her in my mind's eye in her blood-spattered pink suit. It too looked French to me, and I wondered if it was. I made a mental note to find out, and then I realized how stupid that was, how unimportant. Who would care now about the label in her suit, whether it was French or Italian or American? All anyone would know and remember was that the pink wool outfit was soaked with her husband's blood.

I called Marco's room and we made plans to meet in the hotel lobby and go to the office together just in case there was anything more Feingold wanted us to do. I anticipated that the day ahead would be quiet, subdued. Still, I hoped that Ed would have some assignment for me. It would be best to keep busy.

The television station went to a remote from Hyannis, on Cape Cod. A man standing outside the Kennedy compound began a report on the condition of Joseph Kennedy, who had recently suffered a stroke. This could finish him off, I thought grimly, as I walked into the bathroom. I turned on the shower. I lingered too long under the hot, strong water pouring down on me, and I knew I had to hurry if I didn't want to be late meeting Marco in the lobby. I got out of the shower stall, put on a robe and started to brush my teeth.

The commentator's voice on the television suddenly sounded very animated, and I turned off the water running into the sink. The station was going live to Dallas where Kennedy's accused assassin Lee Harvey Oswald was about to be transferred from the city to the county jail. I returned to the chair in front of the television set, my toothbrush still in my hand. I was about to get my first look at a killer, well, an accused killer in any case. Oswald had by this time been arraigned for the murder of a police officer named Tippitt, though not yet for the murder of the American president.

There he was, coming out of the shadows of the basement in the Dallas municipal building, two husky men in plain clothes on either side of him. I was surprised that he was such a small man. His face seemed young, almost like the face of a boy. But as he came closer to the camera I could see he was not a boy. I could see a loose, vapid face of an innocuous-looking man that did not seem to reflect the intelligence necessary to plan and carry out, especially on his own, such an audacious act as the murder of the president. But then, of course, he had been captured very quickly, intelligent enough to commit a vicious act, it seemed, but not enough brains to get away with it. His head is sort of peculiar, I thought, somehow too big for his small, crimped face and his short, slender body.

I heard a popping sound that made me jump. Oswald's face wasn't blank anymore. The mouth dropped open, the placid, empty expression turned to one of surprise. Then the features contorted as though the small, inconsequential-looking man was in pain. He's been shot, I thought. I knew without being told that the popping sound had been made by a gun.

"He's been shot. He's been shot. Lee Oswald has been shot," Tom Pettit, the NBC reporter, said into his microphone, telling me what I already knew. "There is absolute panic. Pandemonium has broken out," he added, his voice reflecting his astonishment, his disbelief.

Tom Pettit's astonishment and disbelief became my own. I sat staring at the screen. Black-and-white images flickered wildly. I couldn't make out what I was seeing. I couldn't comprehend how a man in police custody could be shot so easily. How could someone with a gun get within range of a person so well guarded? How could those in authority allow the man who had killed the president of the United States to be shot? This is ridiculous, I thought, absolutely ridiculous. That popping sound wasn't a shot. I thought it was, but I must have been wrong. Pettit, in the confusion of the moment, had also gotten it wrong. Maybe someone had punched Oswald. Maybe he suddenly got a pain in his stomach and keeled right over. Maybe his appendix burst.

I switched the channel to CBS, the way Ed Feingold had done on the day Kennedy was shot, hoping for some confirmation of the appendicitis attack, hoping for someone who had gotten the facts straight to tell me that the popping sound I had heard was not a gunshot at all and that Oswald was on the way to the hospital to have his appendix removed. But no, Pettit had been right, Oswald had been shot.

I sat down in the chair, my hair dripping water, my toothbrush dripping toothpaste. There was a big blob of blue Crest on the front of my robe. I started to shake. I had known right away what the popping sound had meant, I just didn't want to believe it. I had just seen a man shot, and I felt, somehow, that I had seen and heard this before. I had never seen a man shot before, I had never heard the sound made by a gun, and yet, my God, I had.

I got up and turned off the television set. I no longer wanted to be connected to these events. I no longer wanted to be part of this disaster. I wanted to squeeze the images of people being killed, of men being shot, from my brain. It was too horrible. I couldn't bear such death, such killing. But it was too late. I could hear the popping sound over and over again in my head. I could see the man's face go from blank to anguish again and again. I had heard this popping sound before. I had seen this face before. I had seen such anguish before. I had, at some other time, seen a man falling as a bullet entered his body. And yet, how could this be? I had never before been witness to such a horrible event.

I took off my toothpaste-stained robe and got back under the shower. I don't know how long I stood there with the water beating down on me, hoping to wash myself clean of all my deathly visions. When at last I turned off the water and got out of the shower, I stood within the clouds of steam that the water and the heat had created, and I cried and cried. My eyes were dripping. My nose was dripping. The mirror was dripping. The very air was dripping. Pop. Pop. Pop. A man was shot. A man was falling. A man was killed before my very eyes. My vision was so clear. I couldn't know that Oswald was dead. But I did know that Oswald was dead, as the man in my vision was surely dead.

I put on my robe and, almost against my will, walked to the television and turned it back on. I had not realized that an event could be taped and then rebroadcast so quickly. The murder scene was being repeated over and over, on all three networks. I don't know how many times I saw the man identified as Lee Harvey Oswald grimacing as he was hit by a bullet, but I couldn't get enough. And I was able to listen to the popping sound of the gun over and over and over. But with all the repetition, I still did not understand how I had known at once what the sound signified, it was so small, seemed so innocuous, more like a balloon bursting than a lethal discharge.

Someone was knocking on my door. I opened to find Marco, who appeared out of sorts. I had completely forgotten about meeting him in the lobby.

"Oswald is dead," I said.

"He's been shot. There's nothing yet about his condition. He's been taken to the hospital."

"He's dead," I repeated.

"Well, you must have heard a more recent report since I left my room. I've been waiting for you in the lobby."

"I'm sorry, Marco."

"If he is dead, I bet that's a first, the first time a real murder has been broadcast on television live, so to speak."

"Yes, I imagine."

"You'd better get dressed. I'm sure Feingold is going to want us at the office. God, isn't this unreal? Simply unbelievable. Never seen a man killed before."

"I have. I have seen a man killed before."

"How awful. That's just awful. What a world. What a goddamn violent world all of a sudden. Such madness."

"The world has always been violent," I said with an angry edge to my voice I hadn't intended.

After an exhausting and pointless day in the Cuban community chasing down rumors of a Castro involvement in the killing of the president, in the killing of an assassin who had apparently made a trip to Cuba, we had turned up nothing. I returned to my hotel room early in the evening. I was too tired to eat. I was nervous and irritable. I was homesick. I ordered a carafe of wine from room service and took another shower. I lay down in bed with my wine and watched the continuing television coverage of the world's grief. I was too nervous to deal with my own emotions, so I immersed myself in images on the screen, the drone of endless commentary. There seemed so much to say, and yet, all the words seemed pointless, seemed to afford little solace or comprehension. People were still filing past the coffin, an endless line of people, standing quietly in the darkness, waiting to express their sorrow in a public way. The Capitol rotunda where the body now lay in state would remain open through the night, the commentator informed me, so that as many as possible could pay their respects. I sipped my wine and I closed my eyes. I didn't take in much more of what came from the television, only bits and pieces sank in, and there was little continuity.

Charles de Gaulle had arrived in Washington, and he was going to meet with the new American president. I felt a little less lonely that he was here.

Pope Paul VI warned of the capacity for hate and evil in the world. I was not consoled by this less than original idea.

A reporter in London said, "Great Britain has never before mourned a foreigner as it has President Kennedy." I believed him.

Soviet television was going to broadcast the funeral to its people. How fine that is, I thought, surprised that the Russians would even care about the American tragedy.

A riderless horse was going to be part of the funeral procession, symbolizing that the commander had fallen and would ride no more. I wondered about the origin of such a tradition.

Norman Mailer said, "For a time we felt the country was ours, now it's theirs again." I wasn't quite sure what he meant, but somehow it sounded right.

Assistant Secretary of Labor Daniel Patrick Moynihan said, "I don't think there's any point in being Irish if you don't know that the world is going to break your heart eventually. I guess we thought we had a little more time."

When he heard that Kennedy was dead, Castro said, "This is bad news. At least Kennedy was an enemy to whom we had become accustomed."

"Fuck you, Castro," I said right out loud, using my newly acquired English vocabulary. I was confused about the possibility of the Cuban leader's involvement. Castro and Kennedy were mortal enemies. Castro was ruthless. And yet . . . My doubts just hung in the air. Rumors, even unfounded ones, once heard are difficult to banish.

I couldn't turn off the television. I lay in bed for what seemed a long time watching and listening to the world mourn. Everywhere people were weeping, lighting candles, expressing sorrow, signing condolence books, attending memorial services. They were starting to get on my nerves. You'd think no one had ever been shot to death before, I thought, and was surprised by the bitter feeling behind the thought.

I watched Oswald being murdered a few more times before I fell asleep with the television still on.

I slept fitfully and my dreams were terrible visions, but not of Kennedy or Oswald or Ruby or anything connected with the assassination. I dreamt of a little girl running away from me toward the square of a small town. I called to her, trying to bring her back to me. "Colette," I called, "come back, come back." But she did not hear. Or she could not obey. She kept on running and I wanted desperately to stop her. I knew I had to stop her, but I could not move. I heard popping sounds, pop, pop, pop. I did not know what had caused the sounds, but then again I did know, and I was terrified and helpless before some unspeakable catastrophe which I could not identify.

FONTVIELLE, 1963

7

There was no horizon. The strong blue of the sky melded into the softer blue of the sea. The blending of one shade into the other left no visible demarcation at the line of their joining. I put on my sunglasses against the luminous light that was hurting my eyes. I huddled against the brilliant atmosphere that was hurting my soul. The brightness surrounding me only intensified the darkness inside me.

I had come to the sea for comfort. There were other places to seek solace, but the sea demanded nothing from me, posed no questions, and so, after flying from New York to Nice, this was where I came first to begin the adjustment to my altered circumstances. I had always loved it here at the port of Saint-Tropez. From the first time I had come on a summer outing with my sisters, I had felt happy here, as though I belonged.

Unable to sleep I had come to watch the fishing boats returning at dawn with their night's catch, the wonderful rockfish that finds its way into the big pots of every Provençal household and restaurant, where it becomes part of a soupe aux poissons, a bouillabaisse, or a bourride. The dawn had become full morning, then almost noon, the fishermen had gone to their rest, leaving their nets spread and drying in the sun, and still I sat, staring out across the limitless, listless expanse of blue.

I had to leave, to drive to my home, but I couldn't seem to move from the sea, as though I were still hopeful that it would offer the answers that I sought and I could return to the life I had just left behind. I had hoped that the sea contained God, that the sea contained explanation. But there was nothing other than the water, monochromatic and placid, silent except for the small slurping sound where the water was barred from the land by the stone jetty. Whatever gifts the Mediterranean had for others, nourishment for the body or comfort for the soul, it offered nothing, on this day, to me. I finally rose, turned my back on the parsimonious body of water and walked toward my rental car.

I looked up at the windows of the pink stucco buildings along the inlet and I wondered what the family life was like behind those walls. The home where I had been raised to adulthood was entirely different from the homes where most people live. My family was not a family in any usual meaning of that word. The convent was a singular, female world, with nuns in the place of mothers and aunts and grandmothers, with orphan girls from many different places for sisters. And there were no substitutes for fathers or grandfathers or uncles. I had realized all along that certain elements of an ordinary family life were missing, and I had never minded.

But now, as never before, I felt deprived, for I had had glimpses of another home which had contained all the elements of a normal family. I had little memory of this place, except for a small white-tiled kitchen with a woman in a simple flowered dress sitting at a wooden table cutting green beans into a pot, glimpses of the same woman going about her daily chores and activities. The other memories were of a little girl running away from me into a fog as I called vainly after her, entreating her to stop; a woman lying dead on a street lined with crumbling shops, the earth sopping up the blood seeping from her; a man sprawled against a fence near a gray stone church with no bell tower, his face down, his arms outstretched, dead as I somehow knew him to be. I had come to see these things only recently, since the death of a president, since the death of an assassin. Why was I seeing them now? And the insidious sounds. Pop, pop, pop. Over and over in my ears, the awful popping noises, endlessly. Why could I not silence these sounds that I had never heard before? Except that I had heard that same sound come from the television when Lee Harvey Oswald was killed before my eyes; except that I had heard that same sound coming from the town square toward which the little girl, her dark braids swinging, her arms flung, was running because I, impotent, could not make her stop; except that I had heard that same sound as the man staggered and then fell forward, a grimace spreading across his astonished face, against a fence by a gray stone church.

Everything had changed from the day of Lee Harvey Oswald's murder. The dreams, the visions, the noises in my head dominated my existence. The woman cutting the beans, hanging the laundry, working at a sewing machine—I was sure she was my mother because I felt great love for her. But who was the child eternally running from me? Who was the man against the fence, the woman on the ground, and why had they died in such a terrible way? Where was the small town with its ruined buildings shrouded in fog and its gray stone church overlooking a winding stream bordered by beech trees and hazel shrubs, smoke rising from where I knew the bell tower had once been? Each day more details came to light in my head, and I wanted to know more, as though the answers to my questions would break the dreadful despair that now possessed me and was the abnegation of my faith, that was the denial of my God in whom I had always placed my hope.

I got in the car and drove toward the only place where my questions might be answered. I had been born at a time in which millions all over the world were dying in a war where civilians were slaughtered as readily as soldiers on the field of battle. As an orphan I was no one special. There were too many of my kind. And I had been luckier than most. My parents had died in their beds, of a virulent influenza, too young, too suddenly, but they had not been tortured or brutalized. And I had found a good home with loving people. I had been educated in a classical way, an education not available to everyone. I had been taught to use my mind in the pursuit of excellence, and I had been raised as a child of God. So why dwell on the past, on the loss? Who was I to question God's plan? God moves in mysterious ways, his purpose to fulfill. This purpose would be revealed in God's time and I had been content to wait. But with a sudden pop, a televised murder, my patience was exhausted and I could wait no longer. I needed answers, and I did not even know the questions. I only knew that I had to have an explanation of the images in my head that made no sense.

The wrought iron gate was closed. To the stranger this would seem forbidding, a barrier against the trespasser. But I knew that the gate was not locked, that anyone who wanted could swing it wide and gain access to the gravel driveway that led upward and around toward the old convent complex. I swung the creaking ironwork to one side, then the other, and I followed the way lined with the penitent, ever-faithful cypress trees, bent toward the ground in fealty to the mistral wind that roars its way down the Rhône valley, bellowing past our windows and doors in its determination to reach the Mediterranean Sea from which I had just come. Around the last bend were the honey-colored buildings I had always called home. A homecoming should be a happy event, but it was not to be so on this day. I was here in bewildered flight and sorrowful retreat, hurt and confused, and my family, as is the way, would be sad to see me so.

The convent, run by the order of the Sacred Heart of Jesus, had first been a residential school for girls, then during the war a home for displaced and orphaned girls, then, after the war, again a school as well as a home for those who, like me, were the sole surviving member of their family. Today the convent was a home for the older nuns of the order who had retired from teaching to live out their days in the peace and serenity of this beautiful place.

Peopled with the elderly, the charterhouse had not become a dreary place where life was boring and uneventful, for this order was not silent and contemplative, the nuns trained, as they had been, to be active and collegial and dedicated to working with others. Women such as these would not adjust well to sitting about remembering the past or passing the time that remained to them only in prayer and contemplation. The mothers held retreats, organized benefits, taught the illiterate, tutored children from the town, volunteered in the local hospice. But with their full-time teaching chores put aside, there was, as well, time for the enjoyment of life, which, I had been taught by these women, was as much an obligation to God as self-sacrifice and service to others. Good if plain food, good if modest local wine, books, music, television, companionship, all had their place within these walls, along with the devotion and the meditation.

My arrival was not anticipated and so I walked to the door of the main convent building, lifted the big brass knocker and let it fall against its mounting. The large noise startled me. Perhaps I had never heard it from this side for I had always just let myself in, as one does on entering one's own home. This was my home still, for every orphan who had been raised here was always welcome, for however long, and there were always rooms set aside for us that we might stay whenever we liked. But today I was afraid of startling everyone by my sudden appearance, and so, instead of just using my key, I waited at the door, like a stranger, to be accorded entrance.

There was no response and I wondered if the mothers were away in the town, or working in the groves, or at their devotions in the chapel. I looked at my watch. Not the time for devotions, a schedule I knew well. I was about to raise the knocker again, when the heavy wooden door was pulled open and Mother Gabrielle was standing in front of me, a startled expression peering out at me from the fluted ruff encircling her plump, round face.

"Mon Dieu!" she exclaimed. "Tiens, qu'est-ce que tu fais là?"

I put my arms around the woman who had been in this place since my arrival as a little girl. She held me at arm's length, trying to take my measure, trying to make an accurate appraisal of the state of my being, trying to assess whatever damage had been done to me by the outside world to bring me so suddenly here. By her questioning look, I could tell she had been unable to come to any conclusions. She knew only that she loved me and she drew me into her ample body again, tilted her head to the side to allow for the ruff as she kissed me tenderly on both my cheeks.

"Come, come, my child. Let us find Mother Céline. She must know at once of your arrival." Mother Gabrielle started off down the long hallway, dragging me by the hand as she went her way in search of the woman who was the reverend mother of the convent and who was my mother among mothers, the woman who had been, and still was, the mother to whom I was the closest in love and in confidence. Suddenly Mother Gabrielle stopped dead in her tracks and I bumped right into her. She whirled on me and the familiar scent of incense rose from the folds of her black robes, calming my spirit as though it had narcotic properties.

"Are you ill?"

"No, Mother, I am not ill."

Accepting my word, she turned from me, and with my hand still clasped in hers as though I were once again a little girl, or as though, if she let go of me, I might disappear, she continued in her search for the mother who was in charge of this place. This was the same corridor I had walked in the darkness on the evening of my first arrival with the woman whom we were now searching out, when I thought I had come into the presence of heavenly angels. I felt almost as I had then, lost and afraid and confused. Today I had come of my own accord, purposefully, seeking solace from those wiser and holier than myself, earthbound though I knew them to be, yet still angelic in my perception of them.

We found Mother Céline in her office, not working at her desk on the ledgers that she hated or the correspondence that was often a terrible chore, but standing at the old leaded window staring out on the landscape of soft rounded hills and hard rocky promontories, of wild fields and regimented groves, of ancient trees and newly planted vineyards. When we entered, she turned from whatever thoughts the natural world outside her window had prompted within her, and she said, "Christine, my child, I have been thinking of you and here you are."

"Hello, my mother."

"I'll leave you two alone," Mother Gabrielle said as she closed the door behind her.

Mother Céline came to me, embraced me, not in a perfunctory way, but with her arms wrapped tightly around me. Age had worn deep creases in her dear face during my absence. My gold necklace clanked against the great silver cross that proclaimed her vocation, and she held me fast. The feelings she had for me were not just the love that those of a religious order must, in charity, feel for all human beings, were not just the special sensibility she had for all the children God had placed in her care, but were an emotion more basic and more personal and more deeply felt, that of an earthly mother for a child of her body as well as of her soul. She held my face in her hands, and then, as mothers have done everywhere and in all times, wiped the tears from the face of her little girl. She knew I would not have come if all had been well with me. She knew, of course, when troubled, all children want their mother. She did not know that there were two mothers I needed, the one in front of me, and the one I had lost nineteen years before. Or perhaps she did know.

"What is it, Christine? Come, come, tell me what it is."

"My head. Mother, my head is full of death."

I told Mother Céline what I could about my dreams, about the visions and the noises in my head, but my words were halting, my narrative confused and disjointed. In despair, I fell silent, but when Mother Céline tried to speak, I refused to listen. I was afraid of what she would say, though I could not imagine why, and I pleaded fatigue.

I took my bags to one of the orphan rooms at the far end of the nuns' dormitory. These bedrooms were at the back of the convent, an addition to the original building, and looked out on the flower and vegetable gardens at the near, and the horizontal lines of orange groves which gave us fruit for our nourishment and our delight. At the far, against the sky, rose a medieval hill town, its pastel buildings all jumbled and askew, nestled within the jagged embrace of a rocky promontory. As a child I used to fantasize about what it would be like to live in the town, in a house with a mother and a father, brothers and sisters. I do not remember being envious, only curious.

The orphan rooms were all furnished in the same way, a dresser, a bedside table, a small armoire, furniture hand-crafted by a local carpenter long before the war, as well as a wrought iron bed also made by a local craftsman. Mounted on the wall over the head of each bed was, not a crucifix hung with the tormented body of a god-made-man, but rather a bloodless symbol of the sacrificial event, a simple wooden cross. A plain white porcelain basin and pitcher sat atop the dresser. The only items to distinguish the rooms of the absent orphans from the rooms of the nuns were a bedspread in a brightly colored Provençal pattern, and a mirror which hung over the dresser, for the young girls and the women they had become were permitted a normal vanity, while those who had renounced concerns about their appearance and the impression they made upon others were not.

All the possessions of a personal nature belonging to the orphans had been taken away with them as they went out into the world or had been packed away in boxes in the attic to be claimed at a later date. I thought how wonderful it would be to return to a room that was particularly mine, that reflected the girl who had lived there and contained my youthful treasures and my treasured memories. But my room was barren, stripped of personal possessions and individual meaning. It was a nun's cell, indeed, a place of renunciation and self-abnegation. Except for the mirror, of course, the one concession which I, for the moment, could have done without. The room made me angry. The room made me sad. The room made me resentful. The room made me feel deprived and sorry for myself. For the first time in my life I truly felt like an orphan.

I undressed and crawled under the covers though it was still midday. The bed felt so familiar. I wondered if it was the very one in which I had slept for the twelve years I had lived in this place. The contours of the mattress, the coarse muslin sheets that smelled of plain soap without perfume and of the scented outdoors, and the soft down quilt that had been made during the war by a nun of the convent skillful with the needle, calmed my spirit as the smell of incense had on my arrival and conjured up the serenity and happiness of my childhood. I fell into an untroubled sleep as though I were a little girl again. I awoke to a knocking on my door, Mother Gabrielle bidding me come to supper. I told her I was not hungry, and I fell back into the empty place where I had just been, grateful to return.

Sometime in the darkness Mother Céline came to my room with a tray. As mothers do everywhere when confronted with a troubled, unhappy child, she urged me to eat, hopeful that the food she had prepared would nourish my soul as much as my body. I took some of what she offered, not because I was hungry, but because I loved her and so wanted to please her and ease her anxiety.

I slept through the night and with the early entrance of the bright Provençal light through the small window, I tried to rise to the new day. But my body was lead-heavy, and I fell back against the mattress. I could not envision what the day would contain and so again I slept, eager for extended oblivion. But if my body would not stir, my brain had grown restless. I dreamt, not of the smiling woman in the flowered dress, the fleeing child, the dead man against the fence, the dead woman on the street, but of the places and the people I had just left behind. I slammed Anatole Osterwald's hand in a car door, he screamed out from the terrible pain, but though I pulled and pulled, I could not get the car door open. I knew his anger would be terrible, that he would surely kill me, and I woke gasping. The a cappella female choir lifting its sweet soprano song of praise to God calmed me at once and oriented me to where I was. My room was still dark so I knew the mothers were either at their early morning devotion or the last of their day, the evening worship. I had lost all sense of time, morning melded into evening as the blue of the sea had melded into the blue of the sky, with no line of demarcation to orient me.

"Christine, my dear, we are beginning to worry. You have slept and slept. You must tell me if you are sick. You do not feel feverish, but you must be ill to sleep for such a long time. Christine, please, dear child, wake up a little. Tell me how you feel. Otherwise, I must call the doctor."

"Ooooh, yes, I'm up now, I'm awake. I am sorry if you worried. I was so very tired, exhausted. Working too hard, day and night. The time change. I needed to catch up."

"I have brought you coffee, some bread, and your favorite jam."

"Thank you, Mother. Yes, coffee will be good. My favorite jam. How funny you are. How thoughtful."

"My thoughts are full of you, of what is troubling you, of what I and the others can do to help you."

"Something is happening to me. I don't know what it is, but something strange is happening and I cannot make it stop. Why are some of the memories so terrible? A man shot, a little girl running toward, well, I don't know what, but toward danger, toward something terrible, a woman lying on a street, bleeding, dead. Everyone has nightmares. Maybe that's all they are, nightmares, because I'm tired and homesick, the assassination, so many terrible events. I don't know. But the images are recurring. Over and over. Not everything is terrible. There is the woman in the flowered dress, my mother—I'm sure she is my mother—cooking, hanging out the wash, going to the market, picking flowers from a garden, at her sewing machine. She wants me to remember her. I want to remember, I want to remember her, all about her. I want her back, I want her back. I want a mother in a simple cotton housedress. Oh, I am sorry if this hurts you. You have been my mother. But I want her. I want her back. A mother in a flowered dress. I hate God for taking her away from me and never letting her come back. You told me from the start that she would never come back and at first, you know, I didn't believe you. And then I just forgot her. But I remember her now and I want her back. I want it all back, this other life. I want a father, too. Why can't I remember him? And grandparents. I want grandparents. Did I have grandparents? Did I know them? I want, I want, I want. . . . How selfish I am. How ungrateful. How full of sin. Millions were killed in gas chambers and bombings, and all I know is that I want my family back. My mother, my father, two people out of all those millions. All those Jews. And I don't care. My mother and father are the two I want back. These are the two I cannot forgive. With all that killing, all that horror, how stupid to die in a peaceful place like Limoges, of a stupid influenza epidemic. Influenza! My mother and father are the two I cannot forgive God for taking away. Out of all the millions, it is these two I cannot forgive. And I want a room in a home, an ordinary house. Where is the house where I once lived? What happened to it? I want a room with all my things in it, a room to keep, a room that is just mine, forever, with my dolls and my stuffed animals and my posters and my stamp collection and my movie star scrapbook. I want a room in a house with family pictures on the wall. I want a room. Not this room, this empty, sterile room. Another room. In a house, a normal house. I want a room that is only mine, that will always be mine. I want my home. I want my room. I want my life."

Mother Céline was crying. I had hurt her so badly with my selfishness, my sinful needs, my blasphemy, that I had made her cry. I had never in all my life seen my angel mother cry.

8

I awoke and was afraid. In the dark I did not know where I was. Then the feel of the muslin sheet, so different in texture from the percale I had slept on in America, told me I was in my convent home, safe within the holy sanctuary. But still I was afraid. I had been dreaming of a woman lying in the vegetable garden not far from my window. Her eyes were closed and her skin was as black as an African's. I thought how odd that a Negro woman was sleeping in the garden. There was nothing in the dream that was overtly disturbing, but I awoke in a state of great anxiety as one does from a nightmare.

It sounded like the middle of the night. I know full night at the convent, the particular sounds that can only be heard when the rest of the world is silent—the whoosh, whooshing of the wind in the old eaves; the hoo, hoooing of an owl in a cypress tree; the thump, thumping of ripe oranges falling to the ground in the grove that is but a few yards from my bed; the harmony of the crickets, each playing its own particular instrument within the nocturnal symphony. As I know the night, I know the early morning just before the light of the new day has appeared over the horizon. The darkness of pre-dawn has its different sounds—the chirping of the clicker as the sexton calls the inhabitants to rise from their rest, the creaking of the floor planking as the nuns wash, dress, and move down the hallway on their way to the chapel for first worship, the gonging of the solitary bell from the tower, slow and somnolent, keeping pace with the sleepy women shuffling toward the chapel, the singing of female voices, some clear and true, some disharmonious and strained, but somehow together producing a hymn of praise with a particular beauty. I did not hear any of the new day sounds, and though I concluded that it was the middle of the night, I rose from my bed and padded down the hallway of the old dormitory. I opened the door that separated the sleeping quarters from the rest of the house, carefully latching it behind me lest a draft catch it and bang it shut.

I stopped before the library. I hesitated, then opened the heavy, wooden door and stepped over the threshold into this most wonderful room, the walls lined, from the floor of wide wooden planking to the molding from which the high vaulted ceiling takes flight toward the heavens, with book-shelves crammed to overflowing. As a young girl I had always loved this room, for I was allowed to freely partake of its wonders, to help myself to the precious volumes that told me about the world outside my personal, restricted existence. The room had a special smell of old leather and floor wax and ancient dust released from bound volumes mixed with the sunlight warmth and the perfumed air that gained entrance by the large leaded windows which, except on chill winter nights or when the mistral wind was raging through the region, were flung wide. The smell seemed a perfect blend of the accumulated knowledge of the ages with the sensual abundance of nature.

But this room had not always been a peaceful and musty library. When I first arrived here, and until the war was over, this large room was a dormitory for the displaced and orphaned children, cleared of its worn overstuffed chairs and couches, its long refectory tables and its individual carrels, to make room for two rows of beds each with its own small pine table. But though the room had gained a new purpose, the contents of the shelves had remained in place, and I used to lie in my bed and feel comforted by the books that surrounded me. I used to walk around the room looking at the titles, touching them gingerly with my fingers as though they were treasures of great worth, yearning for all the knowledge and excitement contained therein. As I grew older and taller I had greater and greater access to the shelves, and when full-grown I was tall enough, with the help of the library steps, to reach the highest shelves and was able at last to partake of the books that heretofore had been beyond my reach. I loved to close my eyes, choose a book at random, and delight in the surprise of its contents, a habit that made me into an eclectic reader.

Now, in the middle of the night, the darkness mitigated by the moonlight and the starshine coming through the wavy glass of the leaded windows closed now against the winter chill, I walked up and down the familiar room. I could see myself as I had walked this room for the first time, between the rows of children's beds, Mother Céline holding my hand. I remembered how cool and soft her hand felt, I remembered how big the silver cross she wore around her neck seemed to be as it swung to and fro above my head. "This is Christine of Oradour," she had said to the other children as we went along. "This is Christine of Oradour." I could hear her saying these exact words as I looked up at the high vaulted ceiling, which, as a child, seemed a sort of heaven where, I believed, my guardian angel stood on a cloud and watched over me as I slept. My faith back then knew no bounds.

"This is Christine of Oradour," Mother Céline had said, Christine of Oradour. Of Oradour. Oradour. I came from Limoges. Why then did I suddenly remember Mother Céline saying, "This is Christine of Oradour?" I wondered if my memory was faulty, if I had simply misheard. Did I make up the word Oradour? How could I just make it up? I had to find out if there was such a place.

I turned on a desk lamp and walked to the section containing the reference books. I took down *The World Atlas* and brought it to the desk, placing it under the lamp. I nervously flipped to the back of the volume, to the Index, and I ran my finger down the column beginning with *Ophir, Alaska* until I came to the place where *Oradour, France* should have been, between *Ora, Italy* and *Orai, India*, but *Oradour, France* was not there. I turned to the listings under *L*, ran my finger down the column headed *Lillesand, Norway*, until I came to *Limoges, France* which directed me to *E4 58*. My nervous fingers fumbling, I turned to page 58 even though I knew, since it was not listed in the index, I would not find Oradour on the map of France. I easily located Limoges. I read the names of the towns all about the city I had come from—*St-Junien,*

St-Léonard, Ruelle, Angoulême, Ussel—small places I had never heard of before. I tried some alternate spellings, but still nothing. There was no Oradour, as, of course, I knew there would not be. It was hard to believe that Oradour, if such a place existed, was smaller than *Ohir, Alaska* or *Orai, India* or *Ora, Italy*, and I had to concede that I must have remembered or understood incorrectly what Mother Céline had said all those years ago. I was a child, I was afraid and tired and confused. I was Christine Lenoir of Limoges. There was no Oradour. And yet I knew there was, a place so tiny, so inconsequential, that it wasn't listed in *The World Atlas*, as though it were not part of the world at all, but only a figment of my imagination.

I left the library, again carefully closing the door behind me not to make any noise that might disturb the sleeping mothers. I continued down the hallway to the front door of the building and turned to the left. I walked along the arcade, its archways open to the out-of-doors, connecting the living quarters to the chapel. The long flannel nightdress that I wore was no protection against the chill December air and I began to shiver. My bare feet on the cold flagstone only contributed to my discomfort.

Christine of Oradour, Christine of Oradour was repeating in my head like a litany. I reached the place that was the center of the convent's spiritual life, a place where I had always found solace. The plain whitewashed walls reflected the muted moonshine strained through the old stained-glass windows. The only other light was from the burning candle in the red votive on the altar, its tiny flame telling me that the transubstantiated host was present in the tabernacle. I followed the small, flickering beacon and approached the simple stone altar. The air was scented with the wildflowers in vases by the tabernacle and with the incense still in the atmosphere from the last ceremony when the priest had wielded the censor.

The large icon over the altar is a simple wooden cross, not a crucifix as I had seen in the Catholic churches I had attended in America and Paris. The tortured body of Christ hanging from the cross has always caused me extreme agitation. Of course, the central event of my religious faith is the cruel death suffered by my Savior, but I have always recoiled from graphic renderings detailing the tortures that He endured. The stations of the cross, a devotion documenting the various stages of Christ's journey on the way to His crucifixion, were also difficult for me, but here the stops along the route to Calvary were not marked by depictions of His suffering, but only by a small cross and Roman numerals to indicate the station. I am a cowardly Christian, one who would just as soon avoid contemplation of the realities that achieved my salvation. The Lord displayed in splendor in the golden monstrance is more to my liking. I prefer the glory of God to the gory, bloody sacrifice of the Redeemer. And so the chapel of the convent was my favorite place for worship, there being no graphic renderings of Calvary's highlights on the walls and no bleeding body with thorn-crowned head hanging from the altar cross.

I knelt on a prie-dieu at the foot of the altar where the nuns always kneel for communal or individual worship. Behind the prie-dieu were ordinary pews, such as you would see in any church, for people from the surrounding community and, in former days, the students and the orphans. Anyone was welcome to attend the morning Mass, and I have seen farmers and shepherds and truckers and peasant women and shopkeepers and grape pickers and bottlers and craftsmen and artisans in the congregation, usually wearing the ordinary clothing of their particular métier.

At the moment there was no one. I was alone. All the surrounding world was asleep. I looked up at the plain wooden symbol of Christ's sacrifice and I prayed to be worthy of such suffering. I prayed for explanation of my violent dreams. I prayed for an end to my confusion and my anxiety. I prayed for forgiveness of my sins, especially for having hurt Mother Céline. I prayed for all those who had died during the war. I prayed to be shown the way to a place called Oradour. I prayed, then spent and empty, I could pray no more.

My head reverberated with Christine of Oradour, Christine of Oradour, as though these words were at once a supplication and an answer to my prayers. God was telling me something and I could not understand. I rose from the kneeler knowing I had to find the Christine of Oradour that I had apparently once been. It was God's will that I seek out and find Christine of Oradour, the child Christine Lenoir from a place called Oradour, for only then would I find the answers to my questions and the end to my despair. The way to the future was through knowledge of the past.

I ran back to my room, dressed, packed my suitcase, wrote a short note to Mother Céline that she shouldn't worry, telling her I was going to visit a friend in Aix. I had just asked forgiveness of my sins and I immediately sinned again. I would drive to Limoges on the theory that Oradour must be a section of that city, like Montmartre in Paris, Brooklyn in New York. But Brooklyn has a baseball team and colorful inhabitants by which it is known, Montmartre has the Sacré-Coeur basilica and its resident artists. What claim to fame could Oradour possibly have, that the name of a place rather than the name of my family had been used as my identification? Limoges was at least famous for its porcelain.

I drove away from the convent before Mother Madeleine sounded the cricket that would summon the occupants of the charterhouse to the new day dedicated to God and to man. I stopped the car once at the top of the driveway and looked back at the old buildings turned silver by the light of the moon that was almost full. Then I started on my precarious way, to find the little girl I had been before I had come to the convent, the little girl I knew I had once been in a place called Oradour, for God in strange ways had told me so. As I pulled onto the country road and headed to the nearby town of Fontvielle where I hoped to buy a map before I headed on toward Limoges, the vibrations of the old convent bell reached my ears in the darkness. I knew that the nuns would soon be on their way to worship, and I took comfort from the certainty that the angel mothers would remember me in their prayers, and that the grace earned by their holiness would hold me in good stead as I searched for the place I had been born and where I had lived the first six years of my life.

ORADOUR, 1944

9

June 10, 1944, Oradour-sur-Glane, Limousin, France

It is to be a busy day. A Saturday, there will be visitors up from Limoges to enjoy the countryside, to have a meal in one of the fine local restaurants where the fare does not suffer from food rationing, to fish in the River Glane, to hunt game abundant in the forests. This Saturday is the day for the distribution of the tobacco ration, so many of the farmers and those from outlying communities will be in town to collect their portion. It is, as well, the day for the medical checkup for all schoolchildren in the area after the morning classes. And in the afternoon, there is to be a rehearsal for the First Communion ceremonies to be held in the church the following day. The barbershop will be busier than usual with little boys trying to sit still for the clippers as they will have to sit still tomorrow for the longer than usual church service. Mothers will be coming to town to pick up white dresses and veils and white shirts and knickers from the local seamstresses. Yes, it promises to be an active Saturday in Oradour-sur-Glane. Yet, no extraordinary happening is anticipated, only the usual weekly and yearly events around which the community has always revolved.

And so the inhabitants of Oradour arise this day confident that the ordinariness of their lives will continue. In fact, so commonplace is their existence that they are not even consciously aware of this expectation, even though they, of course, know that an ordinary day in other places during these terrible times is rare indeed. Yet, if there is any place on the shuddering, bloody earth where an ordinary day is still possible, it is in Oradour, a rural community, a remote village in the southwest of France, 12 kilometers north of the commercial city of Limoges. Throughout its long history the town of Oradour-sur-Glane has never been touched by war.

Even now there has been no occupation of this quiet place by the enemy. What would they find here but ordinary people going about their ordinary ways? There has never been a *ratissage*, a raid by German soldiers against French civilians in reprisal for acts of resistance or to search out hidden Maquisards and their weapons. But, of course, there are no members of the Résistance in Oradour, no Maquisards in hiding. And there are no hidden weapons, everyone is sure of that. There are only hunting rifles with the required permits. It is true that there are a few among them who are escaped POWs, a few who are in hiding from the Service de Travail Obligatoire that conscripts able-bodied Frenchmen and transports them to Germany as forced labor. But if the Germans haven't come for them by now, well, it is unlikely they will ever come at all. Most of the citizens have never even seen a German soldier or a member of the Milice, a paramilitary force of recruited Frenchmen used by the Germans to combat local resistance.

Only those few inhabitants of Oradour who have recently come from other places have ever suffered the deprivations of war. Here Limousin beef cattle decorate the landscape. Here the River Glane teems with fish. Here the farms and the small private gardens that are adjacent to almost every home, even those in the town, are abundant with fruits and vegetables. Here the delicious, sweet Limousin peas and the local artichokes for which the region is known are as delicious and plentiful as ever. Here the groves and the vineyards produce ample yields. After all, the sun and the rain and the soil are unaffected by the war.

The Germans are not drawn to Oradour by the attributes of the place, for they do not have time for the delicacies of life. They probably do not even know that the area is famous for its good food, its excellent Bordeaux wine and its Armagnac, or that people come from a distance just to have a fine meal at Milord's hotel and Madame Avril's restaurant on the main street.

Yes, the people of Oradour have known only plenty, and life goes on the same as it always has, in its predictable and pleasant way. The Allied landings on the beaches of Normandy well to the north just a few days earlier brought war as close to Oradour as it has ever been, and the people are grateful, of course, for the wonderful news of the long-anticipated invasion, grateful that those less fortunate than themselves in occupied Europe will soon be free of the hated Hun. They are grateful as well for the few among them who are refugees from places that have experienced the horrors of war—bombardments, starvation, fire-storms, executions, reprisals, impressments, deportations—horrors that most of the people of Oradour can only imagine. But peace would bring no greater change to those who have lived all their lives in and around Oradour than has the war itself. Of course, there would be no more rationing, sugar and tobacco would be plentiful again. But that is the only real difference that the people would notice.

Among the refugees in Oradour there are people from Alsace and Lorraine, territories incorporated into Germany when France was occupied, who refused to live under Nazi domination. There is, too, a Jewish family of five who are living in this peaceful sanctuary under a Christian name after fleeing from Bordeaux when the round-up of Jews for deportation to the East began. The refugees perhaps pray more fervently than the others that God will keep the enemy from their door, for they have seen the evil the Germans have wrought elsewhere. Still, even they who have personal experiences of war, who have more reason than most to be afraid, are no longer unduly concerned. The invasion has come at last, the war will soon be over, the Germans driven back to their homeland over the mountains, a land now in the ruin and the rubble which it only deserves.

So confident are the people of Oradour that their peaceful existence will continue that, while the Jewish family from Bordeaux lives under an assumed name and with forged identity papers at the ready, Monsieur Lévy, the town's Jewish dentist, he who has lived here all his life, goes about his business, as he always has, without giving his ethnicity a moment's thought.

As the new day dawns on this old-fashioned, well-to-do town of farmers and shopkeepers, set on a hillside just above a gentle, slow-moving river that ambles lazily through a landscape criss-crossed by hedgerows and woods, bordered by hazel shrubs and fine old beech trees, scented by the lilac and the broom that grow wild, everything is as it should be, as its people anticipate, peaceful, quiet, ordinary.

The old stone church with its steeple and its squat bell tower stands on a small rise overlooking the bridge across the Glane. At the far end of this bridge there is a station stop for the tram from Limoges. Tracks with overhead lines run between this station and another stop at the other end of the town.

Across from the church are the barbershop and the bakery. From the church the street winds along a rise in the terrain into the town. The main street, named for the current mayor's father, is rue Émile Desourteaux. It is a picturesque street lined with brick houses, lime-washed white or gray, each with shutters in various pastel colors and a small garden in the back, the Hôtel Milord with bright blue shutters and awning against a facade of gleaming white, Madame Avril's restaurant, two dozen or so shops, the mayor's office, a school for boys opposite the tram station and a school for girls in the center of the town. The main street is bisected by a crossroads, one way leads to the town of St-Junien to the southwest, the other way to the Champ de Foire, the village square.

Abbé Chapelle rises from his bed with great effort. He is seventy years old and his health is poor. He dislikes getting up in the darkness as he has had to do since the start of the war which has caused a severe shortage of priests. Abbé Chapelle must walk to Javerdat each morning to say Mass there before returning to conduct the morning service in his own church in Oradour where he has been the parish priest for thirty-three years. It is difficult at his age, and with his arthritis, to make this round-trip journey on foot, but his swollen, painful knees make it impossible for him to pedal his bicycle. The darkness depresses him. He wishes he could wait for the light before he sets out, but then he would be late on his return and the whole day would be thrown off schedule.

Still, things have improved for the old priest, a simple man, a farmer's son. A very devout woman, Odile Neumayer, a refugee from Schiltigheim in Alsace, recently volunteered to be his housekeeper. He had always managed on his own, but older now and in increasingly poor health, he was doing a very poor job of cleaning and cooking for himself. He often went days without a nourishing meal, too ill and tired to make a fire and to prepare the food. Odile had found him one day in a terrible state, ill in bed, his modest rectory rooms cold and in disarray. She had built a fire, cooked a fine, hot meal, cleaned his house, fetched medicine from the pharmacy. She has been his housekeeper ever since, not for pay but in the service of God, in addition to earning her living as a seamstress.

As he dresses in the dark, Abbé Chapelle is buoyed by the knowledge that Odile will have breakfast waiting for him when he has completed his morning services. His arthritis is bad this morning, but Claude Lenoir, the pharmacist, has promised to drop off a jar of a new camphor rub he brought back from his last trip to Limoges. Monsieur Lenoir has heard tell, from his fellow pharmacists in Limoges, that the salve has worked wonders with many of their patients, easing greatly the stiffness in their arthritic joints.

Abbé Chapelle also looks forward on his return to the arrival of Émile Neumayer, Odile's brother, who is attending mission school in nearby Cellule and will be visiting for the weekend. He will help the priest get ready for Sunday's First Communion service, which is a blessing, for there is much to be done yet, decorating the church with flowers, washing and ironing the white surplices, supervising the rehearsal of the children which requires more patience than the old priest can muster. Émile is also going to assist at the Mass, which makes the priest happy. He is very fond of the young, devout Alsatian. His friendship, and that of his sister, have made life for the lonely, overworked cleric more bearable. The refugees from Alsace seem much more devout than the local population, attending Mass faithfully, and Abbé Chapelle has often wondered why this is so. He is sometimes afraid that he has been unsuccessful at his vocation, that it is somehow his fault the townspeople are not regular church-goers. Perhaps he should not have asked them to pray for the Germans whose cities are being bombarded by the Allies. It seemed the Christian thing to do, but, in hindsight, perhaps it was asking too much, perhaps he had been misunderstood. And perhaps they still hold it against him that he had spoken well of the regime in Vichy during some of his sermons. At the time it seemed only sensible that the country try to accommodate to the reality of the German occupation, but it was a mistake, he could see that now. But then church attendance, even before the war, has never been very good. The old women are faithful enough, and everyone wants the sacraments for their children. But the young women, they come only for the special holy days, preferring to shop at the many stores that remain open on Sunday. And the men, well they spend their Sunday mornings chatting and playing cards on the cafe terraces. Abbé Chapelle often feels as though he is a failure.

Abbé Chapelle is not the only one up so early. André Bouchoulle, as always, is awake before dawn to fire the ovens in his bakery. The housewives of Oradour expect fresh bread and brioches and croissants each morning for their breakfast. André's father has been the baker in Oradour for the past forty-five years, but he is old and ailing now, so André and his younger brother Antoine run the bakery. Antoine is late as usual, but André really doesn't mind. He can never get angry at his brother, and he likes being alone to go about his early morning ritual in the old bakery. He loves bringing the ovens to life in the darkness, he loves the sight of the hot orange flames, the sound of the roar that rises at first like a lion awakening and then settles down to a steady growl. André opens the big sack of flour. He will need to get more from the miller at the beginning of the week.

Antoine does not like the bakery. He is only nineteen and will soon begin school in Limoges to become an accountant. He was always good with numbers and loved doing his sums. André's father still works a little, but the old baker is almost eighty-one and his legs and hands, which must be strong for such a physically demanding occupation, are not up to long hours of work anymore. André knows he must marry, and soon, if he is to prosper, a girl who is sturdy and even-tempered and willing to work hard at his side. He already has such a young lady in mind, a farmer's daughter from Orbagnac. Monique is only seventeen, but perhaps in a year André will persuade her and she will get permission from her parents. After all, eighteen is considered old enough to marry in this small farming community. Besides, he knows that Monique hates the farm and wants to live in town.

Antoine enters by the back door. "Bonjour," André says cheerfully, but there is no response from his brother. He looks cranky and out of sorts. It is ever thus and André doesn't take offense. Antoine hates the early morning, so being a baker is certainly not the job for him. Still, once awake, he is a willing worker, perhaps because he knows that in the fall he will be off to Limoges and freedom. "Have some coffee," André says. "The fire is just ready. We should get the first batches in. The sun will be up soon and this is going to be a busy day, I think."

André, an enterprising young man, has decided that he will have sandwiches available on Saturdays for the people who arrive on the morning tram from Limoges for a day in the country. There are always fishermen and hunters and cyclists who might prefer a picnic in the outdoors to a meal in a restaurant. André doesn't much like the people from Limoges. They seem stuck up, like they think they are so much better than the people in Oradour. But so what, he thinks, this is business and he is perfectly willing to take their money. He decides to give the sandwiches a try today because there are also many people expected for the tobacco distribution. Nothing fancy, just his good bread with ham and cheese and butter. He will have to bake extra loaves and he will have to find time to go to the grocer and the butcher. But then, perhaps he will send Antoine to get the provisions. That's a good idea, he thinks, and he smiles as he slides the first batch of bread into the oven.

Doctor Jacques Desourteaux is also an early riser, though he has at least stayed in bed until the sun has risen. There are two patients outside of town he must see today, a dying woman on a farm in La Plaine and a seriously ill child in Orbagnac. He wants to get an early start so that he can go to Limoges by afternoon. He is planning to have dinner with a friend, a fellow doctor also trying to take care of his patients during these times when medicines are often scarce or even unavailable. Jacques is one of four brothers, the third son of Oradour's mayor Paul, who for many years was also the only town doctor until Jacques returned from medical school. Jacques' paternal grandfather, Émile, for whom the main street of Oradour is named, had also been the doctor and the mayor. Jacques worries he will be expected to become mayor in his turn. He hopes not. He has never been as gregarious as his father and grandfather. He prefers to concentrate on treating his patients, leaving politics and the running of the town to others.

Jacques has heard talk of a new drug, penicillin, which is having astounding results in treating the war's wounded. This new drug is, of course, unavailable to civilian populations, and Jacques thinks, with regret, as he goes into the kitchen where his wife has coffee ready, that penicillin could mean the difference between life and death to his young patient in Orbagnac. The children are the ones so difficult to lose. The woman in La Plaine has lived a full life, she is dying essentially of advanced age. But the child, the little boy, if there were only . . . Well, it's no use. Jacques has no effective medicine at his disposal to deal with the little boy's pneumonia. Perhaps he will survive because he is young and strong. Only time and God will tell. Jacques longs for the end of the war, when he will have access to more modern medicines, when he will be able to save those who are lost to him today. He wants to see the miracle cures for himself.

Jacques has often thought of leaving Oradour to practice medicine in Limoges or Avignon or Bordeaux. But his father is seventy-two years old now and no longer able to care for everyone in Oradour, never mind all those in the outlying areas. And so Jacques has never been able to bring himself to leave. He feels too responsible for his friends and neighbors. Then with the war and the Occupation, well, the time for leaving has never come. Still, he dreams of a place where he might practice more modern medicine, a place where he could lead a more stimulating, more sophisticated life than is possible in the town where he was raised. He had a taste of a more interesting existence when he was in medical school at the University of Montpellier, and he has yearned ever since for that life again. But then his wife is happy here, close to her family and her friends, and Oradour is a fine place to raise their children. So Jacques is, by now, almost resigned to remaining in Oradour. All the more reason to treasure his dinners with his old friend from medical school in Limoges, to catch up on the latest in the medical profession. He wants to take the late afternoon tram, and so he must get an early start to visit his patients in the countryside and finish his afternoon office appointments on time. He hopes there will be no emergencies to throw him off schedule.

Denise Bardet has had a restless night. She is a teacher at the girls' school and on Friday she had accompanied some of her students to St-Junien where they took an examination to qualify for higher education. While she waited for the students, she encountered her first Germans, SS troops on their way to Normandy, swaggering about the town. People in the shops talked in hushed tones, people in the streets walked warily and stepped aside, with their heads lowered, to let the soldiers pass. A shopgirl told Denise that two German soldiers had been shot only the day before not far from St. Junien, and that two days before an SS officer, a Major Kämpffe, had been taken prisoner by Résistance forces who waylaid his car and shot his chauffeur. The people of St-Junien, the shopgirl said, were terrified that the SS now billeted in their town would exact reprisals on them for these Résistance activities. In a bookstore two men were discussing rumors they had heard that morning about terrible reprisals taking place in Tulle, a town only 50 kilometers away, because of a Résistance attack on a German garrison. Men were being hung from balconies and lampposts, Denise heard them say, and she shuddered with fright. She had heard tales before of the merciless punishment meted out by the SS in southwestern France, and so she could not discount the rumors of what was happening in Tulle or the possibility that such horrors would be perpetrated elsewhere.

Denise was weak with relief when she finally got her students on the bus, and she didn't breathe easily until they alighted on the main street of Oradour. Her first encounter with German troops had provoked such anxiety within her that she had tossed and turned all night, and so she is weary when she arises Saturday morning. Generally a happy, cheerful young woman, she is worried about the German troops moving north toward the fighting in Normandy, what route they will take. She does not imagine they will ever come to Oradour, but she is anxious about her brother who is attending teachers' training college in Limoges, for she fears the Germans will stop there as they make their way north.

Denise's father was killed in the Great War. She attended the teachers' training college in Limoges and agreed to teach for one year in Oradour even though she is engaged to a young man in Limoges. Her widowed mother manages the family farm in La Grange de Beuil alone now, and so Denise, who could have living quarters at the school in Oradour, goes home to the farm every afternoon. She is very close to her mother and she likes to be with her as much as she can. Denise's fiancé will be coming to spend Sunday with her and she is greatly looking forward to seeing him. He is so sensible, he will surely talk her out of her nerves. As she dresses, she tries to think of being with Lucien and not of the horrible things the Germans have done to people in other towns. Optimistic by nature, she decides the Germans will not stop in Limoges. They will be anxious to get to where the fighting is taking place.

Denise breakfasts on coffee and bread, puts an orange in her knapsack and sets off on her bicycle for Oradour and her morning classes. She turns back and waves to her mother standing in the front doorway. Then she pedals through the quiet, green countryside, enjoying the morning sunshine on her face. It promises to be a lovely day. She is no longer thinking of the Germans. She is thinking of Lucien and of her wedding plans. She decides that she will wear her mother's white dress and veil. She had thought to wear just a simple dress and some flowers in her hair, because, after all, there is still a war going on. But she knows how pleased her mother would be if she were to wear the wedding dress. Yes, it is settled, she says to herself, and feels happy about this decision.

Charles Lévignac is getting ready for school. He is very homesick, but this morning he is happy because his father is coming for a visit. Charles is from Avignon, but his parents have sent him and his brother to live in Oradour until the war is over. His father is an insurance agent and has traveled throughout France for his company. In the course of his travels he had passed through Oradour and he knew it to be an isolated and peaceful place with no railroads, no factories, no

Résistance and no Germans. When the bombardments by the Allies, who were getting ready to land in southern France, began to hit very close to home, Monsieur Lévignac brought his two boys, Charles, twelve, and Serge, sixteen, to Oradour where he managed to find them homes among the local populace. Unfortunately, there was no family that would take them both in, so they had had to separate. Serge is with a farm family outside Oradour, and Charles is staying with an elderly woman of eighty-five and her sixty-two-year-old daughter. The two women are kind enough to the young boy, but it is still a house of old women and he is miserable being separated from his family. He manages to see his brother during the day at school, but still, Charles feels very isolated and very alone. He misses his friends in Avignon, his school. He is going to beg his father, who is coming as soon as he finishes his business in Limoges, to take him back to Avignon the next day. Even if he has to cry, big boy that he is, he'll do it. He feels like crying, he is that unhappy.

Charles finishes dressing and descends from the attic where the old women have made a space for him, just enough room for a bed and a small trunk where he keeps his clothes. He picks at the food set in front of him. He isn't hungry. There is plenty of food here in Oradour. Not like Avignon where his parents worried constantly about getting their boys enough to eat. But what good is the food when he is too miserable to eat? He sets off for school determined to run away, back to Avignon, if his father does not take him home tomorrow. After all, the Germans are moving north now. All the action around Avignon will soon be over. Yes, his father has to listen to him now, even if he has to use tears to make him agree. After all, his mother uses tears with his father all the time to get her way and it always seems to work.

Michel Forest is also a newcomer to Oradour. He had been a law student at the University of Montpellier. But in March 1944 all the universities in southwestern France were closed and then Michel was in serious danger of being conscripted by the Service du Travail Obligatoire and sent to Germany as forced labor. And so his father, a professor of philosophy at the university, had decided to take his family back to his hometown of Oradour where he and his wife still have relatives and friends. They had been invited to stay with the Viscountess of Saint-Venant, a friend for many years, who lives at the Château de Laplaud, near Oradour. Madame Forest's father, the elderly Monsieur Clavaud, who had once been the village teacher, lives with his second daughter and her husband, who both teach at the boys' school and have a house in the town. But they do not have enough room for the large Forest family, Michel Forest being the second oldest of six children. There is plenty of room for them all to stay together in a wing of the Château de Laplaud which is close enough to walk to Oradour. At the westerly edge of the grove, you can even see the town of Oradour lying along a ridge on the other side of the River Glane.

Michel is a very religious and sensitive young man who writes poetry and keeps a notebook full of his observations about life. He has never been certain that the law is right for him, and he has been thinking more and more of studying philosophy as his father had done before him. The closure of the university has given him a chance to rethink his future. For now the life at the château suits him. He loves to wander about the fields and the woods surrounding the manor house. He often sits for hours watching the shepherds with their flocks, the tenant farmers tending to their fields, thinking the deep, philosophical thoughts of an eighteen-year-old. He sometimes feels guilty for his enjoyment of the peace and serenity that surrounds him in this place untouched by war. He prays every day for those who are less fortunate.

Madame Forest, a schoolteacher herself, has taken charge of her children's education which she conducts right there at the château. But the morning has dawned so warm and beautiful that Madame Forest has suspended classes. Monsieur Forest, who must go to Limoges, is taking Jacques and François and Bernard with him so that they may have an outing. Michel has offered to take Dominique to town for a visit with his elderly maternal grandfather and for a haircut at the barbershop so that he will look his best for his First Communion the next day. If Michel can be said to have a favorite sibling it would be his youngest brother, for the little boy is so bright and gentle and affectionate.

Michel and Dominique set out, hand in hand. They walk leisurely, there is no hurry. The little boy from the city loves the new sights of the countryside, the fertile fields, the animals, the birds, the flowers in abundance at this time of year. He delights in everything he sees, and Michel delights with him. As he watches Dominique gather wildflowers for his grandfather, Michel decides then and there to give up the law and to return to the University of Montpellier when it reopens to take a degree in philosophy. His mother, the practical one in the family, may have some objection to this decision, but Michel thinks his father will be well pleased. Bernard is the one in the family to be the lawyer, for he is already possessed of an analytical and precise mind. He also loves a good argument. Michel, for his part, doesn't like quarreling with anyone.

Marguerite Rouffanche is sitting at the kitchen table in her farmhouse enjoying a coffee and a cigarette. Her husband Paul, their son Paul, and their two daughters Amélie and Andrée, who all help with the farmwork at this time of year, have left for the fields. She is alone with her eighty-year-old grandmother and Amélie's baby daughter, both of whom are asleep. Marguerite always enjoys this time to herself before she begins the housework. All is quiet except for the soft snoring from the old lady in the parlor armchair, except for the sucking noises from the baby in the cradle. Marguerite gets up from the table, stretches, stubs her cigarette in the ashtray. She takes one last gulp of coffee and grimaces because it has grown cold. She thinks to reheat it but changes her mind. She wants to finish up her work and get the evening meal prepared so she can enjoy the afternoon. The weather is too nice to spend the day indoors. Later, she decides, she will take the baby in the carriage up the road to see her friend and neighbor Claudette Belliviers. Marguerite is in the mood for a good chat, maybe even a little gossip, and Claudette always knows what is going on both in the farming community and in Oradour. She has lots of family in both places to give her all the news.

Marguerite looks out the kitchen window at the circle of pine trees and the lilac bushes. She smiles. She is feeling happy, though she can't really say why. It is just an ordinary day, but the weather is so lovely that it makes her feel serene. She looks over at the baby in the cradle. What a joy the little one is. Amélie and her husband, who has a furniture shop in the town, are doing well and should soon have a home of their own. But for now they live on the farm and Marguerite is happy to have them. She thought being a grandmother might make her feel old, but no, the baby girl has given her a new lease on life. She hopes that Amélie and her husband will have a home nearby. The countryside is still best for children, she thinks. She smiles again as she starts to wash the lunch dishes. God has been good to her.

Lina Epstein is worried about the medical examination at the school today. She is always afraid that her Jewish identity will be betrayed by someone. She and her family are refugees from Germany and they have been living in Oradour under the name of Durot. Her parents and her brother even go by new Christian first names, their own given names being too Semitic. Her father, David, is known as Louis, her little brother Benjamin as Pierre, her mother, Rebecca, is Isabelle. Lina and her sister Marta were the only ones who seemed safe enough with their real first names. It has been difficult for Benjamin to always remember his new first and last names because he is slightly retarded.

There is no real reason for Lina to be worried. She and her family have been in Oradour for over two years now, and everyone has always made them feel welcome. But she does not believe that anyone knows they are Jewish. She worries that the people of the town would feel differently were they to find out the real identity of her family.

Lina's father has found work with the carpenter Monsieur Beaubreuil. Her mother is a seamstress in a dress shop where they treat her well. Of course, she is very good with a needle, but still, her employer has always been kind to her. Lina tries to comfort herself with the thought that if anyone, knowing they are Jewish, would betray her family, they would have done it by now. Besides, to whom would they be betrayed? There has never been a German seen in the town.

Lina has never completely recovered from the terror of their last days in Germany, from the horrors of Kristallnacht. Her father was accosted in the street that night, beaten up by a gang of brown-shirt thugs. He came home bloody and terrified, and Lina has never forgotten the sight of her father, always so big and strong in her eyes, transformed into a frightened and bewildered man. More prescient than so many others in his position, he immediately began making his emigration plans. It took some doing, but he managed to obtain visas for France. He was successful because he decided at once to emigrate while others agonized about leaving their homes and their possessions and their jobs. David Epstein was leaving a fine position as a mathematics professor at the University of Tübingen, but he knew that his job would be gone soon in any case and so he packed up his family and left. They went first to Bordeaux, but all too soon foreign Jews were being rounded up for deportation. He had one friend in France, Jacob Lévy, a dentist in a small town called Oradour, and Jacob Lévy took them in. When David and his wife found work they moved into a small house of their own and have been there ever since living in peace, waiting for the war to end.

But Lina, still traumatized by Kristallnacht, has never felt secure. An anxious girl, she has, since the Allied landings in Normandy, been more relaxed. But today she feels nervous again. It is the medical exam that has aroused her latent fears, for the doctor will see that her little brother is circumcised. If Doctor Desourteaux did not know before that the boy is Jewish, he will know now, and Lina is afraid that, as the mayor of the town, he might notify the authorities. Of course, she doesn't say anything to Benjamin. She doesn't want to upset him. She doesn't say anything to anyone. She just keeps her worries to herself as she sets out for school with her brother and sister.

It is but a short walk down the street to the school. Lina says good-bye to Benjamin who heads for the boys' school where, despite his deficit, he attends class with the other boys of his age. Lina and Marta enter the girls' school. They wave to their teacher Mademoiselle Bardet who smiles warmly at them. Lina loves Mademoiselle Bardet who has helped her so much with her French, often giving her extra time after school. The sight of her teacher's pretty smile makes Lina forget her worries for the moment.

The sun is high in the sky. People are gathering in the restaurants. Women are seated outside their homes, taking the air, knitting, chatting, enjoying the warmth and the fresh, sweet breeze off the Glane. Christine Lenoir, whose family lives right in town, is walking home from school for lunch. She has just been examined by Doctor Desourteaux who proclaimed her, with a laugh and a tickle, to be a robust and healthy girl. Of course, Christine knew that already. She has never been sick a day in her life. But she doesn't mind being examined by Doctor Desourteaux. He is very gentle and he always makes her laugh with his silly jokes. Christine is walking with her best friend Colette. They reach Christine's door and they part. They will meet again after lunch to walk back to school together. Christine and Colette are practically inseparable.

Christine kisses her mother who is standing in the back doorway looking out at the beauîful day and lost in her thoughts. "Your lunch is ready," she says to her daughter, and the little girl sits down at the wooden kitchen table to eat her ham and butter sandwich. She doesn't even realize that such food is a luxury most people do not enjoy. In fact, Christine has no real awareness that the world is at a war except in a very abstract way. Her mother and father listen to the radio in the kitchen, which broadcasts news of the war, but Christine pays no attention. It all sounds very boring to her, and she will be glad when the war is over, for then, she reasons, there will be no more news on the radio to interfere with the broadcasts of stories and music.

Her mother steps back into the kitchen. She goes to the

stove and stirs the saucepan on the burner. Then she brings the spoon to her mouth to taste the steaming liquid and she smiles with satisfaction. She sits down at the table and smiles at Christine. There is a pile of green beans on the table and she starts to cut them into a pot. Christine chatters to her mother all through her lunch, about school, about Colette, about her medical exam, about her First Communion, about this, and about that. Christine is a chatterbox, her mother always says, knowing full well that the little girl takes after her mother in that regard. By contrast, her father is a reserved person, quiet and gentle. Christine's father is the town's pharmacist. His shop is on the main street of Oradour. The family home is behind the shop and surrounded by a small yard and garden.

Christine's younger brother, Jean-Claude, kicks her under the table. "Stop that, you toad," Christine says and kicks back. "Stop both of you and finish your lunch. This is going to be a busy afternoon. There is no time for foolishness," her mother scolds. The baby, Théo, giggles and squashes mashed peas with his pudgy fingers. Christine makes a silly face at him and the baby giggles again, throws his hands in the air and drops his spoon which clatters on the stone floor.

Christine's father appears in the kitchen doorway. He has been preoccupied lately, worried. He is unable to obtain many of the medicines needed by the people of his town. Even bandages and salves and syrups have been difficult to obtain. He has made many trips to Limoges in search of pharmaceutical supplies, he has consulted with his fellow pharmacists about how best to locate scarce items. Some of his colleagues from pharmacy school are dealing in the black market, but

Claude Lenoir has rejected this way so far. He knows that if the war continues much longer, he, too, may be forced to resort to such means in order to provide for the people of his region. He had thought to discuss this with young Doctor Jacques, but he has not found the moment to bring up such a delicate subject. Claude now hopes that the invasion to the north will make it unnecessary for him to take such a drastic step, and he prays every day for the defeat of the Germans.

"Simone, I am going to bring this salve to the abbé before I open up for the afternoon. I'll be right back," Claude Lenoir says to his wife.

"Why not send Christine? "

"Well, yes, if there is time before she returns to class."

"There's time. Christine, there is a package Papa wants you to take to Père Chapelle. Classes are starting an hour later this afternoon because of the medical exams, so you have time before school. If no one is at the rectory, just leave the package by the back door. He'll know what it is. Now go along, and take an apple, one for Colette."

"Yes, Maman."

"And don't run off with Colette. No going into the woods. Not today."

"The woods?"

"I know you two play in the woods. You'll lose track of the time and I can't have that today. Right after class is rehearsal, and then I need you to help me make a bouquet of flowers for the altar. Oh dear, I wanted you to pick some herbs for me as well. Nevermind, there won't be enough time. I'll do it later. The salve for Abbé Chapelle is more important."

"Yes, Maman."

"Remember what I said about the woods. You've already made your confession, there is not time for another," Christine's mother says with a laugh and kisses her daughter good-bye.

Christine takes the package and heads for the church rectory. On the way she stops at Colette's house to see if her friend will come with her. Colette's mother tells them to go directly to the rectory and then to school. "Yes, Maman," Colette says and she winks mischievously at her friend.

After they make their delivery to the abbé, the two young girls take off into the woods where they often go to play their secret, make-believe games. They have a special place among the trees and behind a big rock that no one else knows about, a place they have hollowed out in a small rise and covered with branches and twigs to prevent discovery. They burrow into their hiding place and, occupied with gossiping and giggling, they lose track of the time, as Christine's mother had feared they would.

The day has grown hot. Hubert Desourteaux is opening up his garage after having lunch with his father at the Milord. The garage has been very busy because, of course, for the duration of the war, everyone has to keep their old cars and trucks and tractors running. No one is able to buy anything new. Hubert is also an automobile dealer, but he has been unable to obtain any new cars for over three years now. Still, his garage has been very busy just keeping the vehicles in the area in running order. Parts are hard to get as well, so Hubert and his workers have been making some of their own. Not long ago he hired a new mechanic, Aimé Renaud, who does wonders with old engines and old parts.

Hubert is the third son of Doctor Paul Desourteaux, the town mayor, and the younger brother of Doctor Jacques. He was happy when Jacques went off to medical school for it relieved him of any pressure to follow in his father's footsteps, to become a doctor as well as the mayor of the town which seems to be a family tradition. Hubert had no desire whatsoever, or aptitude for that matter, to become a doctor. Jacques always excelled in his studies but Hubert was only an average student. He could never concentrate. What Hubert loves is cars. He understands engines, how they work. He can take a car apart and put it back together again better than it had been in the first place. He was instrumental in bringing automobiles and up-to-date farming equipment to Oradour where the population is prosperous enough to afford such possessions. Between the dealership and the garage, Hubert has done well, even during the war. He considers himself a lucky man.

Hubert was once very unlucky, when he went to fight for his country after the Germans invaded. He was taken prisoner and held in a POW camp in Germany for five months where he was worked and starved almost to death by the Boches. He and three of his comrades managed to escape from the camp by hiding in the back of a truck and they made their way by night back to the French border. Resuming his life in Oradour, Hubert has been ever on the alert for any sign of German soldiers, but he has never seen even one—which is a good thing, because he is afraid he would kill a German if he had the chance after the brutal way he and his fellow prisoners had been treated. He had wanted to join the Maquisards, to get back at the enemy for what they had done to him. But his elderly parents had begged him not to go, had convinced him he had done enough already. And so he has stayed in Oradour.

Hubert has recently met a lovely girl from La Grange and for the first time in his life he is thinking of marriage. Now that the Allies have landed and it seems that the Germans will be driven out of his country at last, it is possible to look toward the future. He would like to have a family. He never felt that way before, with the world in such a terrible state, but now he feels very optimistic. After the war there will be gasoline again, and he knows his business will thrive. Maybe it is the fine, warm day, but Hubert, full of Milord's good food and perhaps a little more wine than he normally drinks, is feeling very happy.

The dust is rising from the road. Marguerite Rouffanche looks out her kitchen window and sees, through the pine trees and across the pond, thick whirls of dust coming toward her. She wonders who is traveling so fast. The baby is taking her afternoon nap. Her grandmother is shelling peas at the kitchen table. The rest of the family has gone to the fields. The cloud of dust is coming closer and closer. Marguerite begins to feel a little anxious. She goes to the kitchen door and wonders if she should run to get her husband, but then she feels foolish. It must be Doctor Jacques, she decides, rushing in his Citroën to a sick patient in the countryside. He always drives too fast.

She starts to wash the lunch dishes, and when she looks up again she can see a column of trucks, then a tank with Caterpillar treads, something she has never seen before, within the dust storm. Her anxiety returns. Before she can take any action, the great billowing dust containing its strange procession has stopped right at her house. Soldiers in camouflage uniforms and helmets hold weapons at the ready, pointing them in all directions in a menacing way. Marguerite knows they are German soldiers even though she has never seen one before.

Quickly the troops leap down from the trucks and disperse, rounding up the members of the Rouffanche family before they reach the fields, ordering Marguerite, the old woman and the little baby from the house. The soldiers speak in German but it is clear by their gestures what they mean. Marguerite puts the baby in the pram and wheels it out into the front yard. Then she returns to the house to help her grandmother out the door. Just an identity check, she thinks, and she starts back into the house to get the identity papers but she is held back by a soldier. He gestures down the road. He wants them to go down the road. With the baby pram? With an old woman? He gestures again. Her grandmother looks dazed, confused. Marguerite wants to ask if the elderly woman could remain behind, but she doesn't know any German and so she feels helpless. What do they want with us, she wonders, farmers, women, babies? No one in her family is eligible for forced labor, no one is an escaped POW. But the troops are menacing with their weapons and her fear, as well as her ignorance of the enemies' language, makes her mute. She sees her neighbors, the Belliviers, and the Juge family, including their two small grandchildren, being herded at gunpoint along the road. She does not see the Belliviers' twenty-year-old son. She wonders if he ran and hid, for he is of an age to be taken for forced labor. Why are they still taking young men? she wonders. The war is almost over. Surely the Germans can see that. But at the moment they do not seem to see. Still, they must have better things to do than ordering old people, women, and babies from their homes. There seems no purpose to such an exercise. No wonder they are losing the war, Marguerite thinks with satisfaction.

Marguerite looks around and sees that her husband and children are being marched at gunpoint from the fields toward the road. The sight of guns pointed at her family makes her very anxious.

All together in one close group, the families are ordered to walk alongside the column of vehicles toward Oradour. Before long the men take turns carrying the young children on their shoulders and the eighty-year-old woman on their backs. Along the way other farm families are rousted from their homes and fields and are forced to join the strange procession. Some of the young men, afraid of the Service de Travail Obligitoire, try to run, but they are soon discovered by the troops who search the homes and barns and outbuildings, even the hedgerows, the hawthorn bushes, the haystacks. Marguerite says a prayer that her son-in-law who is at the shop in town will not be taken.

In Oradour many people are lingering over their lunch on this warm and lazy day. Milord's and Madame Avril's tables are still full. In this easy mood, the people look in wonder when they first see the promenade of their relatives, friends and acquaintances from the farms and villages outside town, along with the convoy of trucks and armored vehicles, suddenly appear, coming over the Glane bridge, up the rise, past the church, then down the main street of the town. Women pushing prams, men carrying small children, old folks walking with difficulty, prodded along by SS soldiers. Other soldiers sit on the benches in the trucks and sight their weapons at passersby along the way. At the top of the street the procession comes to a halt and soldiers jump down from the vehicles and begin firing scattered shots at random. The people are more puzzled than frightened. They cannot grasp the meaning of what is happening.

The troops swing into action. Guards are quickly posted at every exit and the town is completely sealed off. About a dozen vehicles halt in the lower part of the town near the church. Three trucks and two Caterpillar tanks drive up to the high part of the town and stop. The mayor is summoned from his office. He has just returned from having lunch with his son Hubert at Milord's, and he is looking forward to a little afternoon nap. But he is brought up short, fully awake, when he is forced at gunpoint from his office and walked to the town square toward which all the inhabitants are being herded.

Things move very quickly now. Everyone who has been out and about, in the restaurants and stores, in the streets, is soon assembled in the Champ de Foire. At the mayor's bidding, on order from a German officer, the town crier starts through the streets beating his drum and shouting for all inhabitants without exception—men, women, children—to go at once to the town square with their papers for an identity check. Everyone is relieved. This occurrence is odd, to say the least, but it is just an identity check, nothing to be concerned about. But Marguerite Rouffanche is concerned. Her family's identity papers are still at home in a drawer.

Colette says to Christine, "I think we had better go. Maman will be angry if I am late for school." "I suppose we must," her friend agrees, reluctantly. They replace the branches carefully over their secret place and head off at a run, weaving in and out among the trees, laughing. Suddenly they are stopped in their tracks by loud popping sounds, sounds they have never heard before. "What was that?" Christine asks. "I don't know," Colette replies. They make a silly face at each other and start off again, anxious not to be late for school. Loud, popping noises. Great rumbling sounds. They are at the edge of the woods now. They scramble up a rise until the main street is in view. They see a strange sight, trucks, giant vehicles, men in odd uniforms of green and brown, holding guns. Instinctively the little girls fall to the ground, anxious not to be seen. Unable to contain their curiosity, they peek again at the scene. A crowd of people is moving down the street. Soldiers are jumping off the trucks, shouting harsh words the little girls do not understand. A white flare is fired in the air, lighting the sky for a moment before fizzling toward the ground. Shots from rifles held aloft by the strange men punctuate the still, warm air, startling the children. They now realize that the staccato popping sounds they had heard before are gunshots, and Christine covers her ears against the unpleasant noise. People are coming from every direction, gathering together, moving toward the Champ de Foire. The town crier, Monsieur Depierrefiche, is banging his drum, but they cannot hear what he is shouting.

Hubert Desourteaux, as an escaped prisoner of war, knows that he cannot go to the town square for an identity check. When he hears the town crier banging his drum, crying, "Tout le monde sur la place," he flees from his garage to his house near the church and hides in a crawl space in his basement.

When the town crier has finished his rounds, SS soldiers are dispatched into all the houses, searching every room for laggards, ordering everyone, even the sick, in menacing tones, to go at once to the town square. "Alle raus!" they shout at anyone who lingers. Those who hesitate are treated brutally, with kicks and blows from gun butts and violent shouting. A paralyzed man who cannot obey the orders is shot on the spot.

André Bouchoulle is rousted from his bakery shop just as he has put some cakes into the oven. He is naked from the waist up and covered with flour. The soldiers do not even give him time to clean up and put on his shirt. He and his brother flank their elderly father, helping him along the street toward the square. It seems they are too slow, and one of the soldiers hits the old man hard in the back with his rifle butt. André, enraged, turns to protest, but his father whispers to him to keep silent. He is not hurt, he insists. Don't do anything to anger the Germans, he pleads. André, as always, obeys his father.

Elderly people are pushed roughly out onto the street. Madame Binet, the seriously ill principal of the girls' school, a coat thrown over her nightdress, is shoved harshly along. All the soldiers perform with precision and effectiveness, without hesitation, as though all had received exact instructions on what they were expected to do.

Christine and Colette see their headmistress being dragged along the street in her nightdress and the cruel sight makes them very afraid. Suddenly, Monsieur Poutaraud, who works at the garage, is running down the street in their direction. The children hear a series of popping sounds, and the man flings his arms as though he might be trying to fly. But his feet stumble, his legs buckle, his face contorts, and he falls, face down against a barbed wire fence. His arms are still outstretched, but if he is winged, it is as a mounted butterfly, a cruciate monarch. Christine cries out in alarm. Colette begins to sob.

The two little girls who know nothing of war recognize war when they see it. They know that the enemy, of whom they have had only the vaguest idea, has come to their town. They run back into the protection of the woods. They fall, they scramble. Colette skins her knee on a rock. Christine feels a tree branch scratch her cheek. They climb the rise to their secret hiding place. They lie, gasping for breath, within the great hole in the earth they have made for themselves and they pull the branches over the opening. They wait, holding hands, their bodies trembling. They speak only in whispers. Their childish giggles have been silenced by a fear they have never experienced before.

Doctor Jacques Desourteaux arrives back in the town from his house calls. He parks his car near the square and he is flabbergasted at the sight of all the townspeople gathered together, and more so by the sight of armed German soldiers. He walks to his father who is talking with a German officer through an interpreter, a Milicien. The officer is demanding that the mayor designate thirty hostages. The mayor, horrified, unable to understand why hostages are necessary for an identity check, draws himself up and replies in a dignified manner that he will do no such thing. If hostages are required, he says, he offers himself and his four sons. Jacques Desourteaux has arrived just in time to become a hostage to the Germans.

By 2:45 everyone has gathered in the marketplace. The Germans proceed to separate the women and the children from the men. The men are lined up in three rows and ordered to

sit down facing the walls of the buildings surrounding the square. They are told that if they turn around they will be shot. The women with their the children are conducted to the church, followed by the schoolchildren who march in long, orderly columns led by the school principal Monsieur Rousseau. A few of the women are weeping but most are calm. From his hiding place Hubert Desourteaux hears the rhythm of the children's wooden shoes as they file toward the church.

The men are divided into groups. André Bouchoulle steps forward and asks, through the Milicien, if he may return to his shop for he has left cakes in the oven. He is told not to worry about it, that it will be taken care of. A Milicien addresses them and says that there are weapons and ammunition hidden in the town by terrorists, and that a house-to-house search will be conducted during which the men will wait in barns and garages to facilitate the operation. The men are also ordered to report immediately if they know where the weapons are stored. An elderly farmer, Paul Lamaud, speaks up and discloses that he has a shotgun for which he has a police permit. The Germans are not interested. The men are led under armed guard to six garages and barns scattered about the town.

Abbé Chapelle shuffles along with the others of his group. He is very tired. He has already walked miles today. His legs feel like lead and his knees are swollen and very painful. The two SS soldiers guarding them do not seem menacing. They are

young. They appear disinterested. They hold their submachine guns easily as though they are sticks of wood for the
fire and not lethal weapons. They do not shout or threaten.

André Bouchoulle is helping to move his father along as
quickly as he can. He would like to help the old priest but he
has his hands full for his brother Antoine has been placed in
another group of men. André is thankful that he, at least, has
been allowed to stay with his father. He cannot see what
sense it makes to be dragging an old man about. The elderly
should have been allowed to remain in their homes.

Abbé Chapelle and the others are taken to the carriage
house belonging to a prosperous farmer, Monsieur Laudy.
The doors are swung open, revealing a space taken up almost
completely by two large carts. The SS soldiers hesitate, seem
uncertain what to do. Then one of the soldiers orders two of
the men to remove the carts, to put them at the side of the
carriage house. When the carts have been removed, the soldiers motion the men inside. The abbé is concerned about
the time all this is taking. He still has many preparations to
make for the First Communion service tomorrow. Still,
Émile will arrive soon and he is such a big help. The abbé is
thankful that Émile is not expected in Oradour until late
afternoon. At least he will be spared this tedious business. As
long as the children are already assembled in the church, the
abbé thinks that he might be able to hold the First Communion rehearsal as soon as the Germans are finished with this
nonsense. It will certainly be too late to resume classes at
the school.

André Bouchoulle does not believe that anyone was sent back to remove the cakes from the oven. It is unlikely that much harm has been done. Some charred pastry should be the only damage, for, after all, the oven is strong, its sides thick and fireproof. Still, the baker never likes to leave an oven unattended after it has been fired. But the day hasn't been a total loss, for his sandwiches sold very well, all that he had made, and he could have sold more. He plans to have more ready on the following Saturday, not just ham and cheese, but a nice variety, homemade pâté and chicken and tomatoes from his garden. André is thinking about sandwiches to take his mind off this stupid affair with the Germans. He is confident that their search will yield them nothing and that they will be soon gone, on their way to Normandy. And perhaps by lingering here instead of rushing to where they are most needed by their forces, the people of Oradour are actually making a small contribution to the success of the invasion. André smiles at this happy notion.

Lost in his thoughts about the First Communion preparations, Abbé Chapelle does not notice when the SS soldiers set up a machine gun and point it at the men packed together in the carriage house. Only when he hears someone, he does not know who, exclaim, "Oh, my God, oh, no, no, God, no," does he realize that the young soldiers, who had seemed so benign, are actually aiming their machine guns directly at him. André Bouchoulle, too, hears Monsieur Moret cry out, "Oh, my God, oh, no, no, God, no." André looks to his right at the man who has spoken, and before he can look again at the soldiers, before he hears any sound of gunfire, his head explodes. His hand flies up to his forehead as though to ward off the blow that has already happened. He does not feel any pain. My father, he thinks, my father. I must help my father. But there is no more he can do, to help his father, or himself. He sees the great fire in his oven roaring to life, orange, hot, huge. *Sancta Maria, Sancta Maria, mère de Dieu* . . .

Abbé Chapelle feels the burning streak of pain in his belly before he even realizes that the soldiers are shooting. He falls to his knees. He hears groans. He does not know if the sound is coming from himself or from another. He doubles over and falls to his side in a fetal position. Another man falls over him. The man mutters something the priest cannot understand but then he is silent. Abbé Chapelle can feel him die. He doesn't know how he can feel this, but he can, for the life leaving a man is tangible somehow. As a priest who has watched many people die, he knows this. The searing pain has spread through his innards. *Sancta Maria, Sancta Maria.* He does not have the time to confront his own death, only his bewilderment that such a horror has happened. He sees the little children, the girls in their pretty white dresses and veils, the boys in their white knickers and crisp shirts, all so innocent, so beautiful, coming to the altar to receive, for the first time, the Lord from his hands. He holds the host with his fingertips and raises it up. *Corpus Domini nostri Jesu Christi, custodiat animam tuam, in vitam aeternam, vitam aeternam* . . .

Jacques Desourteaux is taken, with his father and two of his brothers, to a barn where farm animals have been stabled for the weekend. On orders from the soldiers, he and a young man he does not know lead the two horses and the ox from their stalls to a grassy area in back of the barn. The young man, who tells Jacques is name is Michel Forest, is very upset about being separated from his little brother Dominique who has been taken with the other children to the church. Jacques tries to reassure him that the best place for the little boy is with the teachers and the other children, but the young man still looks worried. No matter, Jacques thinks, this silliness will be over quickly. The Boches will see soon enough that there is nothing to interest them in Oradour and they will be on their way. He hopes he may still make the late afternoon tram to Limoges. Jacques and Michel return to the others and the men take the place of the animals who have vacated the barn. Jacques has a small worry of his own. He has not seen his brother Hubert since the arrival of the Germans. As an escaped POW, Hubert could be in some danger. But Jacques knows Hubert, knows he would have the sense to get out of town and hide in the countryside until the Germans have gone. Surely that is what he has done. No need to worry.

"Maybe we could go fishing next week, Paul," Claude Lenoir says to the mayor, who is standing beside him. Claude is trying to take his mind off the matter at hand and his worry about Dr. Jacques' orders for medicine that have not yet been filled. "We haven't been fishing in a while, and the weather is so fine." "I don't know why you bother to go fishing," Paul answers with a laugh. "You always throw everything back." Claude laughs, too.

The SS soldiers have set up a machine gun and are pointing it in the direction of the men. Suddenly the Germans are laughing and shouting wildly. There is the sound of a shot from the direction of the Champ de Foire, the signal for the firing to begin. Paul's face assumes a stricken expression. "My God, what are they doing?" he says, his voice cracking. Claude turns toward the barn door and sees the machine gun. Before he can comprehend what is happening the soldiers open fire, but they aim low. Claude's legs double under him and he falls to the ground. Both of his legs are on fire. He can't understand why he has been shot in the legs. He hears the other men moaning, crying out.

Jacques Desourteaux also feels his legs go out from under him as though they are no longer a part of his body. But they are very much a part of him as he can feel by the searing pain in his right thigh, his left knee. He throws himself flat on his stomach and hides his head between his arms. He cannot comprehend what is happening. Why are they shooting us? Farmers, townspeople. There is no sensible reason to shoot us. Bullets are ricocheting from the wall against which he is lying. Someone falls on top of him. He is choking on dust and fragments of brick. The Germans must think we are Maquisards. Why do they think this? He feels a trickle of blood but he doesn't know where it is coming from. Men are crying out, calling for their wives, their children, their mothers. Jacques can't call out. His mouth is full of dirt. He can't move beneath the weight of the man on top of him. As suddenly as it began, the shooting stops. Jacques hears soldiers moving into the carriage house, talking, laughing. Above the collective moaning and crying, he hears his father's voice, "Ohhh, my legs, my legs." Everyone seems to have been hit in the legs. The Germans have shot them for reasons that are incomprehensible, and they have shot, not to kill, but to cripple.

A German officer and a Milicien enter the barn. The officer is holding a revolver in his hand. He speaks and the Milicien translates. "Where is the prohibited merchandise?" There is no response, as though the one being questioned understands neither German or French. What prohibited merchandise? Claude wonders. Arms? Explosives? There is nothing like that in Oradour. Claude hears a shot and in an instant he realizes that a man with no answer to the question has been killed. The German moves along, asking the same question of the wounded men at his feet, a question for which there can be no response, and more of his friends and townspeople are dispatched with a bullet. He knows he will have his turn, and he doesn't know what to do. He thanks God that his wife and children are in the church so they can't see what is happening. Surely the Germans will not harm women and children. Why would they? Women and children don't know anything about prohibited merchandise. But then neither does he. The German officer is standing over him. Claude sees the SS insignia on his uniform and he knows that he will be shown no mercy. "Where is the prohibited merchandise?" the German asks in a calm and controlled voice. "There is nothing prohibited in this town. We are only farmers and shopkeepers," Claude says. As the Milicien translates, Claude knows his answer will not satisfy. He closes his eyes. He waits for the bullet, but he does not feel it when it comes. Before his brain shatters he sees the sweet smile of his wife. Her smile was the first thing that drew him to her, and her smile, as now, was always the last thing he saw each night before he fell asleep. *Ave Maria, mère de Dieu, mère de, mère . . .*

Jacques Desourteaux also realizes with horror that the soldier is asking a question no one understands, no one can answer, and the price of ignorance is a coup de grâce. He tries to think what he will say when it is his turn. In his terror he can think of nothing that will satisfy. "Play dead," he whispers to anyone who can hear him. Two more shots and then silence. Jacques hears the barn door close and with a mighty effort he pushes himself free of the man on top of him. He hears the door being opened again, but there are no more questions, no more shots. Something is thrown on top of him. He doesn't know what it is. He feels about with his hand, twigs, tree branches, sticks. Crackling sounds. Heat. God Almighty, they are setting us on fire. Dear God, they are burning us alive. He is filled with a terror he cannot control and he wets his pants. Heat, his shoulder is burning. He lurches up pushing the burning branches off himself with his bare hands. Horrible pain. He cannot stand on his wounded legs. He crawls. He reaches a stall. He tries to climb up, to escape the flames. Everything is catching fire. Thick smoke is filling the air. He climbs the side of the stall, trying to get higher, to get higher, but his burned hands can't hold on. He cares about nothing now, not his life, not his father, not his brothers, not the other men, he wants only to get away from the fire. He takes a big gulp of the smoke, anything to escape the flames. Pain is everywhere in him, and then it is gone. He sees the little boy dying of pneumonia, gasping for breath, his big, sad eyes looking to him for help he does not have to give. *Sancta Maria, mère de Dieu, priez pour nous, priez pour nous, priez pour nous, priez . . .*

Michel Forest is crouched in the corner of an animal stall, weeping, his hands covering his face, his eyes closed tight against the awful sight of the fire, of the men caught in the flames. Screaming, all he can hear is the screaming, for God, for Mary, for wives and children and mothers. Ineffectual screaming. He cannot move. He turns toward the wall and waits for the fire to reach him. His back is arched against the heat, his head is thrown back, his mouth and eyes are opened wide, his fists are clenched, his muscles are tightened, anticipating his agony. He sees his little Dominique, skipping along the country road, a bunch of wildflowers in his hand, smiling in the sunshine, smiling at the day and at his older brother. *Sancta Maria, mère de Dieu, priez pour nous, pour nous . . .*

The Germans are going from house to house, rousting any occupants who have not yet gone to the town square, searching for whatever it might be they are hoping to find. Then they are setting each house on fire. If the sick are unable to leave their beds, they are burned alive.

Instinctively terrified of the Germans, the Epsteins had remained in their home hoping to escape the identity check. Lina Epstein's father, fearing they will now be discovered, gives her the children's forged papers and orders her to hide with Marta and Benjamin under the cement cellar stairs and to remain there without making a sound. Lina tries to protest, but her gentle father is very sharp with her. Angrily, he tells her she must do exactly as he says. With his wife David Epstein waits for the Germans in the parlor, and he calmly opens the door for the SS soldiers. He is holding his and his wife's fake identification papers, proclaiming the Jews to be gentiles, in his hand. As they exit their house, Rebecca and David Epstein know that if their real identity is discovered, they will be killed at once or sent to the East to die. Either way their children will be left orphans. They only hope that the good people of Oradour will care for them.

Two German soldiers enter the church carrying a heavy metal box. Denise Bardet remarks how very young they are, little more than boys. They place the box, from which white cords are hanging, far up in the nave at the intersection of the chancel. A shot rings out from the marketplace signaling for the action in the church to begin. The two soldiers bend over and light the fuse cords. They retreat quickly as thick, black smoke begins to come from the box. Screams of terror rise from the women and children and spread like a wave throughout the church. Mothers beg God to help them, beseech the SS men, who are loading their weapons and unfastening the hand grenades from their belts, for mercy. The smoke becomes thicker. A salvo is fired. A baby carriage is riddled with bullets. A mother drops to the floor dead, her child still in her arms. The suffocating, sickening smoke pours from the box. Women and children flee to the corners of the church searching for air. Some manage to push open the door to the vestry.

Denise Bardet scoops up a little girl in her arms, grabs a boy by the hand and starts to run blindly in a wild attempt to distance herself from the soldiers with the guns and the grenades. She is stopped in her flight by the altar and she heads for the open door of the vestry. The child in her arms is sobbing. The little boy's hand slips from hers. She bends to retrieve it, she reaches all around for him, but she cannot find him for the smoke. He is lost to her. She makes again for the open door and collapses on the floor of the vestry, still clutching the girl in her arms. Denise Bardet looks down at the child. She has not known until now who she is, Marie Tavernier, a child she has taught to read and to write. She is dead. She is limp in her teacher's arms. Blood is oozing from her mouth, bubbling from her nose. The top of her head is an open wound. Marie was to make her First Communion the following day.

Marguerite Rouffanche also seeks shelter in the vestry. Resigned to her fate, she sits down on a stairway, her daughter Andrée beside her. The Germans discover the women who have fled to the anteroom and are furious. They drive them out, shouting and hitting them with their rifles. They fire shots. Marguerite's daughter falls dead beside her. Marguerite drops and pretends to be dead as well.

Denise Bardet, still holding the dead child in her arms, stumbles again into the stone altar where she lays Marie down, like an offering. She looks up at the suffering Christ on the cross and her back is rent asunder. She sees herself in her mother's beautiful wedding dress and veil. She is holding little Marie's hand. The girl is also dressed in a white dress and lace veil, dressed to receive God, to be received by God into His kingdom. She looks like an angel. *Sancta Maria, mère de Dieu, priez pour nous, maintenant, maintenant . . .*

The soldiers are throwing hay, straw, twigs, chairs, over the dead and wounded. The fire is beginning to roar now. Hand grenades are exploding and submachine-gun volleys are ripping the thick air. Marguerite Rouffanche manages to crawl behind the altar. She grabs the stand used for lighting the high altar candles by which she is able to reach a buttress. She pulls herself up toward a broken window and she flings herself out, landing on a grassy shoulder.

Charles Lévignac takes refuge in a confessional where a little boy is already cowering. Charles puts his arms around the child's trembling body. He prays to be pardoned of his sins as he has done before in this place where the priest has heard his confessions and given him absolution. Charles' body is dotted with pain, his leg, his arm, his side. He clings to the child who has gone slack in his arms. He cries for his father, but it is his mother he sees and she is weeping. She thought her son would be safe and now she is desolate. *Mère de Dieu priez pour nous, priez pour nous, maintenant . . .* Dominique Forest hears someone calling for his father but the cries seem far away. He feels a terrible pain in his head, but then he feels nothing at all. He sees his big brother Michel running toward him, across a field of wildflowers, smiling, waving. Dominique knows his brother will save him. *Sancta Maria, Sancta Maria, mère de Dieu . . .*

Hubert Desourteaux hears soldiers entering his house. He thinks they are there to search for him but he is wrong. They are setting all the buildings in the town on fire. Hubert's house is soon in flames and he is forced out into the yard where he hides in a hazel thicket. He is but 150 yards from the church and he hears submachine guns firing, hand grenades exploding. He hears women screaming, children crying, and he can do nothing. He moves to the stairway of an outbuilding and huddles there, on his haunches, his hands over his ears against the horrible sounds. He is filled with despair. *Ave Maria, pleine de grâce, pleine de grâce, Ave Maria, Maria, mère de Dieu . . .*

Fire is raging inside the church. The roof burns through and the arching collapses. The bells melt and fall to the flagstone floor. Those still alive squeeze together. Some try to make it through a small door leading from the side chapel to the rectory but machine guns mow them down. People catch on fire and run like flaming torches setting others alight.

Alphonse Lemartain, from a suburb of Nancy, is a Frenchman conscripted by the Boches when they occupied Alsace Lorraine and incorporated the territory into Germany. He had no choice but to fight as a German soldier because he would have been shot for treason if he had refused, and the Germans would have exacted reprisals against his family. But today he has not obeyed his orders to shoot the civilians in the church, and he is huddled against a wall watching a nightmare unfold before him. He knows if he is caught disobeying his orders, he will be executed on the spot, but he is not capable of shooting women and babies. And in a church of all places. Could there be any worse a sacrilege? Alphonse is not a church-goer, but he is a believer and he knows that his soul will burn in hell if he participates in this atrocity. He is clinging to the wall hoping not to be noticed in all the turmoil. But when he sees the fire spreading, when he sees women and children in flames, he raises his rifle and begins to shoot. He has always been a good hunter, a good marksman, and he aims carefully, shooting to kill in order to end quickly the torment of those being burned alive. He fires over and over, trying to kill as many as he can, until he is driven from the church by the smoke and the falling debris. He stands watching the church disintegrating. The bells fall from the tower, and when they land the ground trembles beneath his feet like the wrath of an angry God. He falls to his knees, coughing and weeping. He begs to be forgiven for what he has done. Alphonse Lemartain does not want to spend eternity in a hell like the one he has just witnessed. *Ave Maria, mère de Dieu, priez pour nous, maintenant et à l'heure de notre mort.*

Marguerite Rouffanche looks up toward the church window from which she has jumped and sees a young woman who has followed her. She stands in the window, holding an infant out at arm's length. She lets it fall. The child screams and the Germans turn at the sound. They fire their submachine-guns at the young woman who falls back into the church. The baby lands in the priest's privy between the chancel and the yard of the rectory with a broken skull and falls down the hole beneath the seat. Marguerite, clinging to the chancel wall, flees toward the priest's garden. She falls several times as bullets strike her. She crawls between rows of vegetables, lies down in a pea patch and covers herself with earth. *Ave Maria, mère de Dieu, priez pour nous, maintenant et à l'heure de notre mort, notre mort, notre mort . . .*

More than a mile away from Oradour a man hears something that sounds like a tremendous scream. A soldier outside the church shrugs. "Kaput," he says and he and his comrades have a good laugh. People in the outlying villages and farms hear shots and explosions. Some hear what sounds like a human cry of anguish, a cry that is so great because it is coming from many, many people.

Christine and Colette listen to the distant sounds that are unlike anything they have ever heard before. They do not know what is happening. They have no experience to bring to bear. They have no basis of reference by which to imagine what the terrible sounds, the great collective moan, might mean. They have no knowledge with which to sort out what their senses are experiencing. They only know that the sounds they have heard and the sights they have seen are strange and terrifying. They are very afraid. They lie in their hiding place and they wait for their world to become again as it has always been. The afternoon turns to silence and, unaware of the absence of sound, they fall asleep. But when they awake, damp and cold, they notice the silence. It is as big and as frightening, in its way, as the earlier reverberations. They do not know how much time has passed, but it seems ages. They peer outside at the light growing dim through the forest canopy. They agree to venture forth.

They run through the trees, instinctively crouched as though expecting some sort of assault. They reach the rise from which they can see into the town. But the town they know is gone. The buildings have turned to smoldering rubble. Smoke is hanging above the empty streets, heavy, gray. Colette starts to cry. "I am going to find my mother," she whimpers, and suddenly she is up, over the rise, running toward the ruins. "Come back, Colette," Christine cries to her friend. "Come back, oh, please, come back." But her friend does not come back. She runs and runs, her arms flailing at the thick atmosphere, her braids flying behind her. Christine does not follow. She is too afraid. She lies on the ground, listening. Her clothes are wet from the damp of the forest floor, and the breeze coming off the Glane makes her shiver. She sees the birds frantically circling above, and even they seem afraid. She hears the barking of a dog. The sound is lonely as it breaks the silence. She wonders if it could be her dog Toby, calling to her, wondering where she is, why she has been gone so long. She wants to run home, but black smoke is darkening the sky and she is too afraid to move.

Solange Tavernier, a farmer's wife, has walked for miles to look for her little girl. She is more and more distraught as she makes her way toward the town, for she hears such eerie sounds and she sees smoke rising in the distance. She reaches the edge of the town where she sees a German soldier standing guard. Trembling, she asks about the schoolchildren, where they are. Now she can see that the whole town seems to be on fire and her distress turns to panic. She is crying. The guard is annoyed. She runs toward him, reaches out her hand, and, as though he thinks she could do him harm, he raises his gun and shoots the young woman where she stands, her desperate questions choked in her mouth, the only answer a submachine gun blast in her chest. Her arms are flung wide and then, as she falls, they are drawn inward as though to protect her broken body from further assault. She sees her husband walking through his fields in the twilight, their little girl on his shoulders, the look on their beloved faces, in the waning light, peaceful and happy. *Mère de Dieu, priez pour nous, Sancta Maria, Sancta Maria . . .*

Mothers in the outlying areas with schoolchildren in Oradour have gathered at crossroads, at the edge of the woods, in neighbors' yards. Everywhere they are frantic, for their children have not come home from school. They have heard noises, but they cannot imagine what the sounds can be. The men in the fields have heard what seems like a strange, low moan and they stop their work, they gaze into the distance, wondering, apprehensive. Anxiety, for reasons no one can explain, is spreading rapidly. One of the farmers, Léon Tavernier, hears a mighty outcry as though it is coming from many voices, a howl that sounds to him like a frantic cry of agony. He hears it so clearly that he is terrified, and he falls to his knees in the field where he has been tending his crop of artichokes. *Ave Maria, pleine de grâce.* As he recites the words he has prayed all his life, thousands of times by rote, but this time with sincere attention as he implores the Blessed Mother for her intercession, he is seized with cold, though the soil on which he kneels, in late afternoon, still exudes the heat it has taken from the sun. *Sancta Maria, mère de Dieu, priez pour nous, maintenant et à l'heure de notre mort. Ainsi soit-il.*

At Laplaud Madame Forest is very alarmed. She does not know why Michel had not returned with Dominique. She walks down the private road leading from the château and out to the edge of the woods. From there she looks down on Oradour. But all she sees is a huge cloud of smoke that seems to be surrounding the town. Others join her, worried about their children. They tell each other that it is the woods at the other side of the town that are burning. Even if it were Oradour, they are certain that the town would have been evacuated. Madame Forest returns to the château and Madame de Saint-Venant tries to ease her friend's fears. Suddenly they hear a huge, ungodly roar. Madame Forest rises from her chair and calls out for her children.

The killing and burning that was begun at half past three is over by five o'clock. The destruction of the town and its people has been accomplished quickly as though all had been thought out and planned very carefully.

Monsieur Lévignac is on the tram from Limoges. He promised to visit with his sons Serge and Charles before returning to Avignon. On the same train is Professor Forest and his three children who are returning to Laplaud after their day in Limoges. The little train is clattering along slowly over the narrow-gauge track. A few kilometers outside Oradour a man comes alongside on a bicycle and shouts to them that the Germans are in Oradour and have set the town on fire. He warns them not to continue on. But the motorman, determined to keep to his schedule, refuses to stop. Monsieur Lévignac and Professor Forest are suddenly very frightened. Madame Forest is waiting for her husband at the Laplaud tram stop. She tells him that Michel and Dominique have never returned from Oradour. The Forest children get off the tram, but their father decides to continue on to Oradour to look for his missing sons. It is now about 6:30.

At the station just outside the town the tram is stopped by German sentries. Soldiers enter the cars and demand to see papers. The terrified passengers can see the town and the church burning, soldiers tossing grenades into houses. All those who are from Oradour are ordered off the train. The rest are told to take the tram back to Limoges. Monsieur Lévignac, frightened for his two sons, gets off at La Plaine, the second stop on the return trip. Professor Forest gets off at Laplaud and walks to the château.

The Epstein children have not been discovered in their hiding place under the stairway, but at dusk the heat from the fires drives them from their house. They hear the terrible sounds of the crackling flames, they smell the gasoline used to intensify the conflagration, and they see thick smoke hanging all about them in the waning light. Before they can think what to do, an SS soldier wearing a long camouflage cape and holding a rifle sees the three children. The soldier draws his open hand across his throat. This is a gesture the Jewish children have seen before and they run, as fast as they can, into the fields. The soldier does not pursue them.

Professor Forest, waving a white handkerchief, approaches the guard in the lower part of town a little after seven o'clock. He says, in German, that he has come to look for his children. The SS man tells him that all the women and chil- ·

dren have been sent off into the woods where they are safe.
Professor Forest can see the flaming church from where he is
standing. He reluctantly turns away from the terrible sight
and starts to walk back to Laplaud, hoping that his two sons
have made their way through the forest back to the château.

In La Grange de Beuil Denise Bardet's mother cannot
understand why her daughter has not returned. She has
heard nothing of what is going on. Late in the afternoon her
son Camille arrives from Limoges, but he doesn't know anything either.

The news that Professor Forest has brought from Oradour,
that the women and children are in the woods, is beginning
to spread throughout the countryside. Many who are waiting
for the return of their loved ones begin to search the woods.
They shout, call out their children's names, but there is no
response. Some carry blankets and thermos bottles filled
with hot drinks, for it has turned very cold.

By ten o'clock every building in Oradour but one has been
burned to the ground. The house still standing belongs to
Monsieur Dupic, a dry goods dealer. A prosperous man, he
has a fine wine cellar, and his larder is full of foodstuffs, so his

house has been used by the Germans as their headquarters. When evening comes and the killing and burning have stopped, the survivors hiding in gardens and beneath piles of stones and in thickets hear singing and laughter coming from the Dupic house where champagne from the wine cellar is fueling a drunken celebration.

Christine Lenoir, shivering on the ground, cannot understand these new sounds, singing and laughing, accordion playing. Merry sounds, happy sounds. She thinks she has been dreaming. She thinks that she has fallen asleep and has had a terrible nightmare. She is full of the relief that waking from a nightmare brings. She rises from the ground and heads toward the town, toward the laughter and the singing. She knows her mother is going to be very angry with her, but she doesn't care. Even if she is punished, she just wants to go home. She starts to run. Then she sees the horror that the day has wrought emerge out of the darkness, and she knows it has not been a nightmare after all.

As in many of the houses in the countryside and small villages, no one is sleeping at the manor house or in the surrounding homes of the manor's tenant farmers. Some pray. Some weep. Madame and Monsieur Forest sit together in Dominique's bedroom looking at his empty bed.

By five o'clock in the morning Professor Forest, frantic now, returns to Oradour. He asks a sentry where the children have gone. The sentry replies, "Alle kaput." Impatiently he shoves the professor away and holds up his weapon. Professor Forest, in an agony of despair, turns and starts back to Laplaud. On his way he meets Louise Bardet who is headed into town to look for her daughter, and he warns her not to go into Oradour for she might be shot. As Professor Forest approaches the château, he does not know what he will say to his distraught wife.

By dawn Monsieur Lévignac has made his way back to Oradour where a sentry bars his way with shouts and threatening gestures. Frightened, he retreats and goes instead to the farm where his older boy has been staying. It is empty and looted. He hopes his son has made it into the woods and he leaves a note on the farmhouse door against his return. "Dear little Serge, I have been here and am looking for you. Father."

For a third time Professor Forest walks down the hill to Oradour. Trucks full of singing SS troops pass him on the way, going in the opposite direction. One of the soldiers throws an empty champagne bottle out of the truck and it lands at Professor Forest's feet. Crossing the bridge he approaches the town and he can feel the heat and smell the stench from the smoldering buildings. He approaches a sentry and again asks about the children. The soldier becomes enraged and tells him he knows nothing about any children. He threatens to treat Professor Forest as a partisan unless he gets out of Oradour. As Professor Forest again heads out of town, he sees a little girl wandering about aimlessly. He tries to approach her but she runs from him, toward the woods. He thinks he should go after her, but he is in such a state of despair over his sons he just stands and watches her disappear among the trees.

Indeed, despair is spreading throughout the countryside. The people watch helplessly as the motorized columns move along the roads away from Oradour. The last SS troops drive away from the ruined town about eleven o'clock on Sunday morning after setting fire to the last house, belonging to Monsieur Dupic.

Christine Lenoir is wandering about the streets of the town. She does not comprehend the sights that she sees, the smoldering remains of buildings, the ruins of the church. She is choking on the stench of the air. She looks down at the ground and she sees a woman lying there, covered with dirt.

Her skin is dark, brown as the soil. She seems to be asleep. The little girl wanders on. She sees another woman lying on her back. Christine has never seen death before but she knows that the woman is dead by the large bloody wound in her chest and by her eyes that are wide open and empty. The ground all about her is dark and wet. Christine heads toward the main street and she stops by the body of Monsieur Poutaraud hanging from the fence. She walks from one side to the other, looking with wonder at the lifeless man, his wavy black hair fluttering in the breeze, his arms out-stretched like one who has been crucified, outstretched like the arms of Christ on the cross over the altar in the church where she is, in a short while, to make her First Holy Com-munion.

Christine wanders on toward the river. She remembers that her mother wanted some herbs, and Christine knows that she will find herbs aplenty along the riverbank.

In La Plaine where, after fleeing from the town under the cover of darkness, he has taken refuge with the family of his mechanic Aimé Renaud, Hubert Desourteaux watches the German procession pass. The trucks are loaded with booty. The SS men are singing and drinking and playing accor-dions. At intervals some of them aim bursts of submachine gun fire at the houses where people huddle in terror and at the startled animals in the fields.

Hubert sets out for Oradour in search of his father and his brothers. On his way he meets up with Monsieur Lévignac and they enter the town together. Hubert goes directly to the ruins of his garage where he finds blackened bodies, the limbs contorted as though the dead are still seized with terror and pain. He backs away in horror and he brushes up against one of the bodies which crumbles and disintegrates into cinders. Hubert does not know if his father or his brothers are lying dead before him, but he falls to his knees and weeps uncontrollably as one would who has lost all of his family.

Monsieur Lévignac makes at once for the church. He enters and cries out in horror at what he sees before him. Burned bodies that seem still in the process of horrible writhing are everywhere. He frantically begins to search for his sons, peering at the stiffened faces, one after another, wherever there are recognizable features. Behind the altar he finds the blackened bodies of many children all fused together by the heat of the fire into a horrific sculpture. He sees a dead infant in a baby carriage riddled with bullets and the body of a little girl untouched by the fire lying on the stone altar which is intact. He cannot find anyone recognizable as his sons, and he feels a small hope that they have somehow escaped.

Others are entering the church to search for their loved ones. Mothers are weeping and wailing. Léon Tavernier bends over a small body, reaches out his hand as though to caress it, and the child breaks apart, blackened limbs falling from the torso. He does not know who the child is, but, in a paroxysm of grief, he pulls at his hair and digs his fingernails into his face. His cries of agony rise through the air now perfumed with the unholy incense of fire and death toward the unpitying sky, the brilliant blue, where the church roof had once been, mocking his uncomprehending grief with its clarity and its calm. He turns and walks toward the altar where he finds his own child with the top of her head blown away. He makes not a sound. He picks her up and lovingly carries her from the church.

Unable to bear these sights any longer, Monsieur Lévignac flees the church. He hears a small cry of distress and he finds Marguerite Rouffanche in the pea patch. At first he thinks she is a Negro, though he has never seen a Negro in Oradour. He looks more closely and he sees that the woman is not a Negro at all, but is badly burned and covered with dirt. He calls to Hubert Desourteaux for help. Marguerite begs them to throw her into the Glane, she does not want to live. She has been lying in the garden for almost twenty-four hours. She has heard the Germans talking and shouting, singing and laughing as though what they have done to the people of her town, to her loved ones, is a joke. The men put her in a wheelbarrow and take her to Laplaud. She is silent, she does not say a word until they reach the château. Professor Forest bends over her and she tells him that all the women, all the children were burned to death in the church. Professor Forest begins to weep. Marguerite Rouffanche cannot weep. She has lost her husband, her children, her grandchild, all of her family, and she cannot weep. She does not know why she saved herself.

Léon Tavernier carries his daughter all the way back to his farm. His house is empty. He does not know what has become of his wife, but he fears the worst. He buries his child in his fields under an aged oak. Then he begins the long walk back to Oradour in search of his wife.

The Epstein children, who had wandered during the night out into the countryside, in the light of day are taken in by a farmer and his wife to whom they relate the terrible events they have witnessed. They have lost both of their parents, not because they were Jews, but because they happened to be living in a town called Oradour on a day unlike any other.

In Oradour, under the brilliant blue sky, the first day of a world now altered forever has begun. People, dazed, their faces reflecting anguish and resignation, search the ruins for their missing loved ones. Civil defense workers, who arrived at first light, are trying to help the survivors identify the dead, a task that, in most instances, is impossible.

The swallows are flying about in confusion looking for their nests that are no longer. Iron signs still identify buildings that are now only empty shells without purpose. Dogs cower beside their former houses waiting for their owners to return. The yards and streets are swarming with domestic animals. Pigs, ducks, chickens that were released from the barns before the doomed men were put inside wander aimlessly about the streets as though they do not know what to do with their freedom. A few cows return to their burned out stalls where they lie in the ruins.

A civil defense worker cries out with horror when he finds the charred remains of a baby in the oven of the Bouchoulle bakery.

Christine Lenoir is standing in the shell of her father's pharmacy. Her paternal grandfather and an uncle lie dead in the Desourteaux garage, her mother and her two little brothers, her grandmothers, her aunts and cousins, are burned beyond recognition in the church, her father is dead of a coup de grâce in a barn, her maternal grandfather and another uncle have been burned alive in a carriage house. Christine walks about, stepping over smoldering debris. Glass crunches under her wooden shoes. "Toby," she calls, "Toby." She does not call out for her father, her mother. Perhaps she instinctively knows they are dead. But she has seen dogs waiting for their owners. The Germans did not kill the dogs, the animals of the town. Only the people.

"Toby," Christine calls. "Toby." She picks up a bottle that is completely intact, still holding its liquid medicine. She puts it down on a piece of wood, carefully, not to break it. Her father was always very careful with his vials of medicine. She steps over the bricks that had once been the back wall of her father's pharmacy and she walks out into the front yard of her home. "Toby," she calls. "Toby. Come, Toby. It's me, Christine." Climbing over the crumbling ruins that had once been the front wall, she enters the parlor. She stumbles over some bricks, and breaking her fall, she cuts her hand. She sees the sewing machine with which her mother had made her First Communion dress and veil lying amidst the rubble of the parlor. It has fallen from the little upstairs sewing room to the floor below. She makes her way to the kitchen. The cast iron stove is where it always has been, almost unscathed. She can see her mother standing there, at the stove, stirring the cassoulet in the big pot she always used to prepare this dish, one of Christine's favorites. Christine sits in the ashes and the mortar and the debris that her kitchen has become. She burns her leg on smoldering cinders. It is here that a civil defense worker finds her, sitting, holding one of her mother's pots in her lap. The civil defense worker sees that the pot contains green beans. When she tries to take the pot away from the child, to lift her up out of the rubble, Christine screams and refuses to let go of the handle. The kind young woman tries to calm the little girl. She lets her keep the pot and she carries her from the ruins.

"Have you seen my dog?" Christine asks. "His name is Toby. I must find him. I must find him. He will be afraid without me." Christine calls, "Toby, Toby, viens ici, Toby. C'est moi, Christine."

The civil defense worker is crying.

"I am going to make my First Holy Communion today. Maman has made my dress and it is very beautiful."

The civil defense worker looks in the direction of the church where smoke is still rising from the hallowed ruins.

ORADOUR, 1963

10

Tombeau des 642 Victimes du
Massacre d'Oradour S/Glane
Souviens-Toi

The words at the top of the memorial exhorted me to remember. To remember—the purpose that had brought me to this place. I ran the tips of my fingers over the letters carved in the stone, letters forming the names of my family members. I knew that one of the names, Simone Millay Lenoir, was my mother, another, Claude Auguste Lenoir, my father. I could remember a little the faces of my parents, the aura that they had possessed, the attributes that made them unique. I could feel a little the love I had borne them and they me. But there were so many others, lost relatives I had long ago forgotten as though they had never existed. The length of the list took my breath away.

Alphonse Lenoir
Ariane Sonnier Lenoir
Auguste Lenoir

Charles Auguste Lenoir
Charlotte Pruneau Lenoir
Claude Auguste Lenoir
Edouard Lenoir
Hélène Marie Lenoir
Jean-Claude Lenoir
Monique Claire Lenoir
Simone Millay Lenoir
Théodore Lenoir
Théodore Millay Lenoir
Valmore Lenoir

In addition to these names I had to assume that those listed under my mother's maiden name were somehow related to me as well.

Denise Fontaine Millay
Melina Millay
Cathérine Dalmason Millay
Philippe Millay
Frédéric Millay
Gérard Millay
Marie-France Millay
Marcel François Millay
Madeleine LaBranche Millay
Alexandre Millay
Rodolphe Millay

So many among the 642 victims listed on the monument that somehow belonged to me. I had never realized that names can evoke so much meaning, especially when carved into the stone of such a memorial to the massacred as the one before me, for that at least acknowledges people's existence and attests to the wrong that was done to them.

In the deep recesses of my soul I believe I had mourned my mother and father. But I had had no awareness, until now, standing in the ruins of my childhood, of the extent of my loss, of the monumentality to which my grief was entitled. To suddenly see in the stone how many had been taken from me in such a horrendous way, how truly aggrieved I was, seemed overwhelming. I did not even know exactly who these people had been to me. Grandparents, uncles, aunts, cousins? And yet my sorrow became tremendous as it expanded to include all my relatives and indeed all those who had been my townspeople—friends, neighbors, teachers. I had never undergone the grieving process, and now it seemed that only great weeping and lamentation would be appropriate to the deprivation I had unwittingly suffered.

When I left the convent I went directly to Limoges. In a bookstore I purchased a guidebook and a map of the city, but I found no mention of Oradour. "Please, can you tell me, is there a section of the city called Oradour?" I asked the clerk in the bookstore. "No, no," she said, "not in Limoges. There are two towns nearby called Oradour, Oradour-sur-Vayres and Oradour-sur-Glane. You probably want Oradour-sur-Glane. That is where the visitors go, to the ruins where the Germans killed all those people during the war. That is only a short drive or tram ride from here."

I knew without hesitation that Oradour-sur-Glane, "where the Germans killed all those people during the war," was my destination. I inquired of the shopkeeper if she had any books about the wartime events in Oradour-sur-Glane to which she had alluded, and I purchased everything she had in the shop on the subject—*Oradour-sur-Glane, Vision d'épouvante, Larmes et lumière à Oradour, Oradour, Le crime—Le procès.*

I bought some bread and cheese and pâté, a bottle of wine, and I took a room in a small hotel on the outskirts of Limoges. I read into the night until I finished the three books I had purchased, and by the dawn of the new day I felt I knew what had really happened to my mother and my father. They had been massacred, along with almost everyone in the town and many from the outlying areas, men, women and children, by the Germans, either by bullet or by fire, on June 10, 1944, for reasons that still remained obscure. The SS troops may have mistaken the town of my birth for Oradour-sur-Vayres where there had been Résistance activity and were looking for a cache of weapons. They may have been looking for a German major who had been kidnapped by Maquisards on a road not far away from Oradour-sur-Glane and who had been a friend of Major Dieckmann, the officer in charge of the massacre. Some have said they were after a shipment of hijacked gold. Or, perhaps the events were just a mindless, senseless atrocity of World War II perpetrated by SS troops trained for brutal acts of reprisal against civilian populations and under the command of officers who, facing the certainty of defeat since the Allied invasion, were exacting a dreadful revenge that their vision of world domination had been thwarted.

It was the middle of the afternoon before I arrived in Oradour-sur-Glane. December, the winter light was already fading. I approached a man in a Ministry of Culture uniform. "Please, may I see the monument to the dead before it gets dark?" I inquired anxiously. "I am just going home," the old man said. "Oh, please," I begged. "If I may see the monument for a moment, I would be very grateful. If you could just tell me the way." After all the years, I felt I could not wait until morning to verify that this was the place my parents had lived and died, that their names were on the monument I had read about as I was almost convinced they would be. Even to find my mother and father on such a list of the doomed seemed better at that moment than a continuation of the uncertainty. The old man hesitated, and then, probably sensing the urgency as it came from me, relented. "Very well. Follow me. It isn't far. But just for a few minutes. No one is permitted after dark, you understand."

It was but a short walk, past ruins that were only benign silhouettes in the fading light, until we reached the monument erected to the memory of those who had died in the massacre situated at the place of the mass grave where those victims, charred beyond recognition, had been buried. When I found my family name on the stone memorial to the people who had been killed on June 10, 1944, in this town that was now a shrine, all the buildings preserved as the Germans had left them, in ruins, on that fateful day, I was overcome with sorrow, but I knew that I truly was, as I had somehow understood, Christine Lenoir from Oradour-sur-Glane.

Shivering with the damp cold coming on the breeze from the River Glane and with the fear that I would never remember the portion of my life I had lived in this place, I thanked the attendant for his kindness and proceeded to the new town of Oradour that had been built to replace the one that had been destroyed. Hoping that the light of day would illuminate my memory, I took a room at the Hôtel Milord.

I was not afraid of what I would find in the ruins of the town. I was afraid of what I would not find, memories of the place and its people, of me within the existence of a small, peaceful farming community in southwestern France before it was unaccountably extinguished by brutality and fire. I was afraid, too, of the anger within me at the ones who had deceived me. The women who had raised me from the age of six had dedicated their lives to God and so to truth. But they had failed in their vocation for they had raised me on lies. It was startling to realize, for the first time, that nuns could be sinful, deceitful, less than holy. My mothers at the convent had always been perfect in my eyes, angelic, full of grace. Now, as the moment comes for every child, but for me, at age twenty-six, later than for most, I realized that the people who had raised me to adulthood were, after all, only flawed human beings. Because my adoptive parents had been nuns, garbed in robes and veils, bejeweled with the cross of Christ, dedicated to the worship of God and the betterment of mankind, it was harder for me than for most children to accept parental weakness and duplicity.

The morning arrived cold and damp and overcast. I returned to the ruins. Guidebook in hand, looking for all the world like an ordinary tourist, I made my way about the ghostly town. I saw no other visitors. It was not the time of year for vacationers, so close to Christmas, the weather gray and chill. I was glad to be alone. It would have been disheartening to see holiday-makers, no matter how respectful, strolling about, taking photographs of my personal disaster.

I stopped at the entrance gate. A notice I had not seen the day before read, *Le temps est resté figé pour que tu te souviennes,* again an exhortation to remember, and I was so afraid I would be unable to comply. Another notice told me that anyone was permitted entrance during daylight hours, with no payment required, and requested of visitors a respectful demeanor and correct attire.

I passed the ruins of the church without stopping. I did not yet feel strong enough to enter the remains of these ancient walls where, my reading had told me, my mother had probably died along with most of the women and children. As I made my way along the main street, following the tram line, nothing about the place seemed familiar. I tried to visualize the daily life that had been described in my books, but it was difficult. Each burned-out, roofless, windowless building was identified by a small plaque—the post office, the bakery, the grocery, the barbershop, the butcher-shop, the dressmaker, the pharmacy. The pharmacy! I had been told by the nuns that my father was a pharmacist in Limoges. Perhaps there had been some truth in the information they had given me, perhaps my father *had* been a pharmacist, not in Limoges, but here in Oradour. My heart was pounding.

I peered inside but there was nothing recognizable within the battered walls, nothing to reveal the place it had once been. My eyes searched for something from my past, of my father, but there was only debris and ruin. I walked around back, across a yard, and stood in front of another burned-out building. A water pump stood by the garden gate, reminding me how simple life had been in this place.

This had been my home. I had lived here. I knew this, not from any memory of the place, but because the sign told me it was the pharmacist's house. My father's house. And so my house.

No one was about. I thought to step across the threshold where the front door leading to the rooms within the now crumbled walls had once been, even though I knew this was forbidden. I changed my mind, not wanting to disturb the design of the interior, the testimony to tragedy that the precise arrangement told about the day of fire as it had ended. The home was mine, the tragedy was mine, and still I did not have the right to trespass. It would be wrong to disarrange any element, no matter how small, that belonged to the history of the place, to its life and to its death.

Again my eyes searched for something familiar, any clues to my past, but all I could make out was a battered cast iron stove where the outside back wall had once stood. This far room, on the other side of the parlor, would have been the kitchen, just off the back garden, and this the stove on which the pharmacist's wife, my mother, made meals for her family, for me. The sight of the lonely stove made me feel desolate. I tried but I could not see the woman in the flowered dress standing there, putting something to bake in the oven, checking something cooking on the burner. The place was too desolate, too broken, to envision a normal life taking place within its confines, to visualize something as commonplace as a woman at her cooking.

I walked on a little farther, keeping to the main street, until I came to the ruins of the mayor's office and the site of the school for girls where I probably had attended classes.

Then I turned and headed back the way I had come. The place was absolutely silent, still. There was no life here. There was no memory of life. I was walking quickly now, anxious to be gone from this dead place. I saw the man in the Ministry of Culture uniform who had kindly permitted me to see the monument the afternoon before. He smiled at me and I smiled back, but fearing he might stop to talk, I lowered my head and hurried on.

Returning to my hotel room I thought to leave the following day. This place was not going to help me. I couldn't remember anything of my life here. My amnesia seemed such a terrible rejection of my family. This ruined town did not speak to me of the way they had lived but only of the horrible way in which they had died. Yes, I would leave here tomorrow, I decided firmly. Where I was going, I did not know.

That night I dreamt of the sweet, smiling woman in the flowered cotton dress. She was seated at a sewing machine, bent over a piece of white lace, intently working the material in and out, around and through, the pulsing needle, her foot rhythmically pumping the treadle, until, beaming happily, she held up her finished work, a beautiful wedding dress.

I did not leave. My dream bade me stay. My dream told me that that which was lost, while scarcely known, was not lightly missed. I remained for many more days walking all about the town, all about the surrounding countryside. I was no longer trying to remember. I could see that was pointless. I just allowed myself to wander through the present, to notice what I would, to take in whatever presented itself to my senses. It was a comfort to feel the breeze off the Glane, to look on the rolling hills and the aged trees, the high green meadows and the chestnut plantations, the red dairy cows and the Limousin cattle in the pastures, to listen to the rustle of the pines, the flow of the river, the clack of the tram, and to know that these were the same breezes my parents once felt, these were the same sights my parents once saw, the same sounds they once heard. The consolation I did not find in the ruins of my town, I found in the natural world, which changes little in such a remote area, as though some elements of my family remained in the air and the water and the land.

On the fourth day of my stay, as I had just started up the main street of the ruined town, the man in the Ministry of Culture uniform came upon me unawares.

"Bonjour, Madame," he called out to me.

"Bonjour, Monsieur," I responded and continued to walk on.

He came alongside me. "You have been here awhile, now," he said. "You come each day. If you have any questions, please do not hesitate to ask me. Or if I can be of service in any way."

"That is most kind," I responded, "but I have my guidebooks." I felt almost annoyed, as though he had been spying on me.

"I can tell you things you will not find in any guidebook."

I didn't know what to say.

"You lost someone here, I think."

"Yes, I lost someone."

"May I inquire?"

"My parents."

"I lived here at the time. Perhaps I knew them."

This was so unexpected. The man I had assumed was just an employee of the governmental department in charge of maintaining such memorial sites might have actually known my mother and father. I just stood staring at him. I had been learning about the way my family had died. Here was someone who might be able to tell me about the way my family had lived.

"May I know your name?" the old man asked, gently but with expectation.

I hesitated, fearing disappointment. "My name is Christine Lenoir."

At first the wrinkled, weathered face in front of me remained still and blank, but within a moment all the features realigned themselves into a portrait of joy. The thin, dry lips widened, the ruddy cheeks rose. Lines formed all about the small black eyes and ran like little streams into the deeper crevices that extended downward to the corners of the upturned mouth. The surprise and happiness that was the man's face seemed to presage great whooping and hollering, but the sounds that came forth were but a whisper.

"You are Christine, little Christine. Claude's little girl. Simone's. My God, my God."

"Yes, yes, I believe that I am."

"Oh, you are. You are. I can see this, I can see this. You are their daughter. I can see this, yes, without doubt. I can see them in you, your mother's eyes, her mouth, your father's chin. Just look at that chin. His curly hair. Oh, yes, there can be no doubt. I knew you had lived. But then with all the grief, all the confusion, I did not know where you had gone, what had happened to you. And here you are. From out of

nowhere. I have lived to see you again. Little Christine come
back to Oradour."

This man knew me. This man knew my mother and
father. This nameless old man had just confirmed, if there
had been any lingering doubt, that I was, in truth, Christine
of Oradour.

I spent many hours with the old man during the following
days. His name was Léon Tavernier and he had been a
farmer, as his father and grandfather had been before him.
On June 10, 1944, his wife and his only child, a daughter, had
died. The little girl was killed in the church with the other
schoolchildren. His wife, who had become greatly worried
when she had seen smoke rising from the distant town, had,
unbeknownst to her husband who was still working in the
fields, walked to Oradour. Léon was told by a survivor who
had hidden in a thicket near the church that when she got
close enough to see the town in flames she had panicked and
she had run wildly toward an SS soldier who had shot and
killed her. After the war, when the ruins of Oradour were
made an official memorial site by the French government,
the grieving man sold his farm, took a room in the new town
and became the caretaker of the place where his family had
perished. He spent his days giving tours, making sure the
lawns were mowed and the bushes trimmed, that the crumbled buildings were clean of trash and debris, that the visitors
treated the place with respect and decorum. An uneducated

man, he was learned on one subject, the town of Oradour-sur-Glane before and during the infamous day of its destruction. He knew at least something about every name on the memorial monument, and, like any good historian, he knew the events of June 10, 1944, what had happened, when and where, the actions of the participants—the dead, the survivors, the perpetrators.

Léon and I walked together, sat together over coffee in the morning, pastis or a beer in the afternoon. I told him about my life since I had left Oradour. He told me about my life before I had been taken away. He stood with me in front of the memorial, pointing to the stone names of those who had been important to me, family, of course, but also the teacher who had taught me to read, the doctor who had brought me into the world and had cared for me once I had arrived, the priest who had baptized me and had prepared me for my First Communion, had heard my first confession, the baker who had made our bread, the grocer who had sold us our provisions, the vintner our wine.

Léon told me that Ariane Sonnier Lenoir was my grandmother, Auguste Lenoir, who had been a bookbinder, my grandfather. Auguste had prospered before the war and had a shop both in Oradour and in Limoges. Cathérine Dalmason Millay and Alexandre Millay were my maternal grandparents, Alexandre having been a printer. He told me who were my aunts and uncles and cousins. He told me a little about each one, their appearance, their personality, their foibles, their attributes, as much as he knew. Valmore Lenoir, my father's older brother, had fought and been gravely wounded in the Great War. Melina Millay, my mother's younger sister, had been a maiden lady, a woman of great independence and good humor who had never seemed to mind her spinster state and who had been a fine pastry chef at Madame Avril's restaurant. Edouard Lenoir, my father's youngest brother, an extraordinarily handsome man, had run away to Paris to become an actor, but unable to make his living on the stage had returned home and had gone to work for his father in his print shop. But he had never lost his sense of the dramatic, always doing everything with a grand flourish, and, always in love with the theater, he had directed the plays and pageants at the town's schools.

Most startling of all, Léon told me, pointing to the letters in the stone that read Jean-Claude Lenoir and Théodore Millay Lenoir, that I had had two younger brothers, Jean-Claude, age four at the time of his death and Théodore, called Théo, age two. I had never imagined, for the nuns would have surely told me a thing of such importance, that I had had two brothers. Brothers! It seemed an extraordinary concept. I had had sisters at the convent, but the revelation that I had had brothers of my own blood, of my own birth parents, was such a gift and such a loss at the same time that I could not manage my conflicted feelings at the news.

My people, maternal and paternal, had not been of the land, had not been farmers or grape-growers or cattle ranchers. They had been shopkeepers, craftsmen, artisans, cooks, and teachers. My father had, indeed, been a pharmacist. And so they had all been townspeople, those who had both lived and worked within the town of Oradour-sur-Glane. And so they had all been killed.

"Your mother was a pretty woman. Small, dark—well then, almost everyone around here has dark hair and eyes. She was plump. Well, after three babies what can you do? That is only natural. But she was pretty, pleasing to look at, a fine smile. I would say she was a happy woman. Yes, I can safely say that. And your father, he was quiet, serious, so different from his brother, the actor. We were in the same grade in school, your father and I. We made our First Communion and Confirmation together. We were married about the same time, he was at my wedding, I was at his. Claude was always a good student, not like me. He went to study in Limoges and when he returned he opened the first pharmacy we had ever had in the town. He was very serious about his business. Not just the money, I think, not just to make the money, but to take care of the people. Of course, I did not see your family often. But we came to town every market day, to sell our produce, to buy our provisions, and from time to time we would meet, at the market, along the street, and have a little chat about this and that. I remember once my wife was ill with fever and I went to your father late in the evening for some medicine. He was not angry or irritated at the late hour. He was only concerned and very kind. Your mother, she had the prettiest garden, the prettiest of the whole town. I remember this. There were always pretty bouquets of flowers from her garden in your father's store and on the altar of the church."

"If it is not too painful, I should like to know about your wife and your little girl."

"I never thought to be so fortunate in a wife. I never imagined that a girl like Solange would consider me, a simple farmer, for a husband. The happiest day of my life was the day we were married in the church, with flowers and music and friends. It was like a miracle. She wasn't a beauty, I suppose, not like some of the other girls, but she was a—I don't know how to say, she had a way about her. She was a strong girl, stubborn, too, and willful, but strong and eager, I think you would say, eager about life, and a companion, a fine and loving companion for my days, the days we had together. Our daughter was a bonus, a happiness. Some men want only boys, but I was happier to have a little girl, soft and gentle, not like so many little boys, rowdy and rough. She loved to hug and kiss her papa, yes she did. You don't get that so much with a boy, I think. My two girls were everything to me. I had the farm, the long days, the hard work, but it didn't seem so hard, I was working just for them. I am luckier than others. I still have possessions, objects that belonged to them, I still have photographs to look at each night."

"Photographs. Oh, how wonderful. To have photographs. May I see them sometime?"

"Of course, I would be pleased to show them to you."

"Why did they do it? Why? The war was coming to an end. Why would they kill the people in a small town, the children? What was the purpose?"

"I do not know. No one knows. The German officers in charge were either killed before the war ended or were never found. The trial of some of the soldiers after the war proved nothing. Many were Alsatians who claimed they had been forced by the Germans into the SS, that they had to do as they were told or be shot. They feared reprisals on their families back home in Alsace which had been incorporated into Germany at the start of the war. No, the trial was a farce. Many reasons have been suggested for the tragedy. Some have even said there was stolen Nazi gold hidden in the town. But none was ever found. Even if there had been gold or weapons hidden here, members of the Résistance, why kill all the women and children, the old, the sick? Why? I say it was just evil run amok. The men who were tried were apathetic, like robots, without remorse, like machines. All their humanity had been rooted out of them by the SS training. They claimed to know nothing, as was usual. They said they just did as they were told, as was usual. I went every day to the trial, and I watched them, the soldiers. They had dead eyes, dead faces. There is no answer. There is no explanation for such evil. Do not look for one." Léon paused and took my hand in his. "Now, what about you? What is next for you? It is almost Christmas. Surely, you are expected at the convent for Christmas?"

"I do not want to go there just now. I am still too conflicted about my feelings, about all the lies."

"You must not stay here too long, Christine. You must not stay too long. I have never gotten beyond this place. My grief has never permitted me to get beyond it, to go away perhaps, to begin again. But you, you are young. It is a fine, fine thing that you have returned, that you have learned what you could of your family. But it is time for you to go along, to take what you can from Oradour, and to go along, to live your life. This is a dead place, my dear. A dead place is fine for a visit, to remember, to pray, and to grieve, but it is not a place for life. It is only a place of life that is past and gone, it is a memorial."

"Soon, I'll go soon. Yes, of course, I'll go soon, you'll see."

But I made no plans to leave. I did not know where to go. I could return, with my anger and my hurt, to the convent, to those who had deceived me, not knowing what I would say to them. I could return, with my confusion and my grief, to New York, to my job at *World* where they had granted me a sabbatical. I could lose myself in work and in the anonymity of the city where no one knew anything about me.

I lingered. I hesitated. I wandered still. I poked and prodded my memory with the sights and sounds, to little avail. I floated aimlessly, from here to there among the ruins. *Le temps est resté figé*, as the sign at the entrance to the ruins said. The time was fixed that the event would be remembered. My life, too, seemed fixed, but in a time and a place that I could not remember. Léon, the caretaker of the past, watched me in my madness without admonishment. He had told me it was time to go and then, patiently, he simply waited for me to follow his advice.

I had a dreadful nightmare. It was a crucifixion, but it was not an image of what is commonly portrayed, the Christ hanging from the cross. This was a Christ hung wrong-way-round. As Saint Peter had been crucified upside down, this man was crucified backward, facing the wood of the cross, and so from my view an anonymous man, an anonymous martyred man. The next day I told Léon my dream. He pursed his lips. He squinted his eyes as though he were trying to see the image I described.

"There was a man, he was shot by the Germans as he tried to run away, shot in the back. He fell face down against a fence, his arms outstretched. He remained so all the day, the Germans left him hanging there. I saw him that evening. A young man. His arms outstretched, like on a cross, backward."

"Would I have seen this?"

"I do not know. It is possible. I was told you were found wandering. It is possible that you saw. What a terrible thing for a child to see. But then nothing was too terrible on that day."

"Take me to the fence."

I stood looking at the fence upon which the poor young man, a mechanic at the local garage, had hung, and I could see him there, his hair caught by the breeze. I had seen him against the fence, and I had seen him as he had been shot all those years ago, and again in a vision when Oswald had been killed. It was that vision that had begun my journey to this place. Then I had forgotten again, my mind closing over what it did not want to acknowledge. I had forgotten, but my dream had remembered for me, a cruciform image, graven deep in the brain matter, set before my eyes in my sleep, the dream version remembered now in my wakefulness. The nuns had told us that Christ is crucified each day by sin, and on that day long ago, it seems I had seen sin made manifest with my own eyes.

At last I decided on my destination and I set the day for my departure. I would return to the convent the day of Christmas eve. Amidst the hectic preparation for the ritual of Christ's birth there would be no opportunity for discussion, for dredging up the past, for recrimination. I would make up more lies to account for the time I had been gone, I would tell Mother Céline what a good visit I had had with my friend in Aix. I would stay at the convent through Christmas day and then depart on the 26th for New York. I would be returning to work is all I would say to Mother Céline and she would accept that. I would never mention Oradour. I would tell her I was feeling so much better, that all I had needed was a change of scene, a rest. I would leave, and things between us would remain as they had always been, predicated on deceit. Why dredge up the past at this late date? A woman of God, Mother Céline's motives, of course, had been good. She had done what she had thought best. And she was old now. Magnanimously, I would forgive her.

On the day before my departure from Oradour, I said to Léon, "It is time for me to visit the church."

"I'll leave you to go on your own. I'll wait for you in the museum. The church is a place best visited alone."

I stood within the ancient walls and looked up at the overcast sky that was now the building's only roof. This was the place where 300 women and 205 children had died. This was the place where my mother and my two younger brothers and my grandmothers and my aunts and my cousins had died. This was the place I should have died but for some fortunate happenstance. What that lucky turn of events could have been, I did not know, nor did Léon.

I had, thus far, avoided the church for fear it would overwhelm me. It did not. Not at first. It did not seem a place where hundreds had died. It seemed but an ancient ruin, such as one might see from the Middle Ages, from the Greek and Roman empires, a ruin made from the passage of time and the inevitability of decay that is the fate of all earthly things. It did not seem the recent ruin that it was, destroyed but a few years before by man's brutality, out of the basest impulses of which human nature is capable, a bestiality I had been taught was part of all human beings but which could be controlled by attention to God. Grace, I had learned as a child, made man transcendent over the evil portions of his nature, but grace, it seemed, had not won out, even in a church where grace was dispensed in the confessional, was made visible in the Mass, was received in Holy Communion, on the day when the roof of this once holy place fell in on my mother and my brothers.

Though I tried, I could not imagine what it had been like for my mother—the flames, the bullets, the crashing bells, the falling stones, the inferno, the horror, the pain, the crying of her terrified, doomed babies—or perhaps God, in His mercy, would not allow me to imagine. I prayed, as I stood looking up at the sky, that they had died quickly. But if there had been such a mercy, I would never know.

I approached the altar, which was almost intact. At just about the place where the faithful would have knelt to receive their Lord in Holy Communion, there was a rusting pram riddled with bullet holes. This might have been Théo's pram, mine and Jean-Claude's before him. This might have been the exact place where Théo died, of bullets rather than fire as I wanted to believe. Again, I would never know. The ruins no longer seemed ancient. It was as though they had been formed only yesterday. It was as though the dead had been massacred only a few hours ago. I touched the pram with my fingertips, and I fled.

I found Léon in the little museum by the cemetery where the artifacts of daily life in Oradour that had survived the holocaust were exhibited like relics. I had already seen the wine glasses, the spectacles, the equipment belonging to the Jewish dentist, the watches with broken faces all showing mid-afternoon times when they had come to a stop, a sewing machine with a treadle that was labeled as belonging to the pharmacist's wife. But now I saw something I had not noticed before, a pot, just an ordinary saucepan, but with a dent in its side.

"This was my mother's," I said to Léon.

"It could have been, I suppose," he said. "These objects had been brought here before I arrived, before I became the caretaker. The museum was already as you see it. Not everything was labeled as it should have been, so it is possible the pot was your mother's."

"No, no, Léon, I am certain of it. This was my mother's pot. I remember the dent."

I picked up the pot and put my arms about it as though it were an infant child. I rocked back and forth as though the object that I held had need of comfort. Now I could see the woman in the flowered dress standing at the cast iron stove in a white-tiled kitchen. The pot I was holding was on a burner. She was stirring the pot, then she was bringing the spoon to her mouth, tasting the steaming liquid, smiling with satisfaction. She replaced the lid, she sat down at the kitchen table, and she started to cut green beans that were piled in front of her into another, larger pot. Her dark hair was wound into a knot on the top of her head. Her eyes were as large and black as olives. She wore a gold band on her left hand. She wore tiny gold earrings in her ears. She had a dimple in her left cheek when she smiled. She was buxom. The flowers on her dress were yellow with green leaves against a background of white. There was a tiny line of perspiration on her upper lip. There was a small gap in her upper front teeth that only enhanced the warmth of her smile. I had never seen so many details about the woman in my dreams of her. But now, suddenly, holding the pot that had belonged to her, I could see her ever more clearly and the clarity of my vision, of what I had truly lost in her passing, made me cry, something I had not done since I arrived in Oradour. Seeing my mother as I did in that moment, I began to truly grieve for her. I had never known before how much I had lost, all that I had missed, when she had been taken from me.

"Oh, Christine, my dear. Oh dear, oh, dear," Léon wailed. Not knowing how to comfort me, he said, "Take the pot, my dear. Keep the pot. It is yours. Oh, dear, oh, dear, take the pot with you."

"No, no, Léon. The pot belongs here. The pot must stay here to remind people that there were loving women living in Oradour who made meals for their families, who raised their children, who lived good lives. No, the pot should stay here where it belongs." I replaced the cooking implement back in the place where I had found it among the relics.

Early the following morning I made my departure. Léon kissed me and said, "Do you think you might write to me, just a note from time to time, to tell me how you are, what you are doing?"

"Of course I shall write you."

"That would be a pleasure for me if you did."

"And I'll come back for a visit."

"No, no, do not come back. There is nothing more for you in this place. Go, have a good life. Live to the full the life that was spared."

Live to the full the life that was spared, he had said. I didn't know how to do this. It was as though I owed Marie Tavernier and all the lost children of Oradour a perfect life of great accomplishment and worth to make up for their lives that would never be lived, and I wasn't even sure where I was going after I left the convent.

"Do not come back here again," Léon added.

I couldn't bear the finality of his words. I wanted to be away quickly then, suddenly realizing I would probably never see Léon again. I turned the key in the ignition, but Léon, with a look of surprise on his face, started to speak again. I turned off the engine.

"I just remembered something. Your little friend, your best friend. You were always together, your dear friend, oh, my old brain, I cannot remember her name. She survived too, you know. You did know. No, you didn't know? She went to live with an aunt and uncle in Limoges. I don't know anything beyond that, but if you want, I could try to find out where she is. If I could remember her name. Never mind, it will come to me. If I just let my old brain rest a bit, it will come to me, probably in the middle of the night."

"Her name is Colette." The name surfaced in my mind, not out of a memory of my best friend, but out of the dream I had had about her, running away from me, running away when I didn't want her to go, not even turning when I called her name, begging her to come back. "She had long braids."

"Yes, yes, of course, Colette. You remembered. Yes, she had long braids. You two were always together. How fine. Colette. Colette Orrefort. You see, I told you I'd remember. I'll write you at the convent if I find out where she is. She came back once. I remember now. To see to her family's property."

"Her family's property?"

"Her father was a prosperous man. He was a lawyer with a practice in Limoges. He lived in Oradour but he went by tram each day to his office in Limoges, not such a long journey. I think when Colette returned after the war, she had a lawyer with her, surely someone who knew about financial matters. Of course, your father was properous too, the only pharmacist for miles around. Not rich of course, but substantial. He also had a little vacation house just near Saint-Tropez. Nothing grand, he told me, but in such a nice place for the August vacation. Do you remember? Your father said that children were always well-behaved at the seashore. The house, right near the water, must have brought a nice amount. And then your grandfather, the bookbinder, he did very, very well with his business, especially at his shop in Limoges. Very well, indeed. He had people come from all over France for his services. He was a real artisan. As the only living member of your family, you must have inherited a tidy sum. I'm sure the convent took care of all that for you."

"Yes, yes, they did, of course."

"There should have been an account for you."

"Oh, yes, of course, there was. An account. Yes, certainly, I received an account."

"Well, there then. Colette Orrefort. I'll find her for you, Christine, shall I? Yes, that would be a wonder for you, to see your friend again."

"It would be fine, indeed, Léon. Let me know what you find out."

"Go now before you see me cry. Good-bye, dear, dear Christine."

"I am so grateful, this you know. Good-bye, Léon."

"God bless you and keep you on your way," were the last words Léon said to me.

It was hard to believe that Léon still had faith in the God whose name he invoked. We had never spoken of God's place in the events of Oradour. For myself, I had lost my faith in an instant, standing in the ruins of the place built for God's worship, praying that my mother and brothers had died a fast and merciful death, when I saw the bullet-riddled pram. It seemed almost a physical act, my renunciation of God. I could feel myself laying down my faith in His goodness by the pram next to the altar behind which the charred bodies of many children, no one could say how many of the 205 children killed that day, welded together by the heat into one grotesque entity, had been found. Man had killed these children as God had watched and done nothing. I felt my faith fall apart, disintegrate into charred remnants as the bodies had done at the touch of those who had come to the church searching frantically for their loved ones.

I had more questions than answers as I left Oradour. If I had hoped that my visit would achieve a resolution of some kind, I had been wrong. There was no way to leave the matter of my origins unresolved with Mother Céline. There were even more reasons for confrontation. If the lies had been told to spare me the knowledge of the terrible events in Oradour, that was, in a way, understandable. But what had become of my family's money, my family's property? There was a business in Limoges and a house near Saint-Tropez. I had never known. I had never been told about any account. Perhaps the money from my family had been used to defray the cost of my upbringing, my education, and that would be as it should be. But at least I had the right to know that I had not been a destitute orphan, that I had not been a charity case, that my father's hard work had provided for me, and that his dreadful death had earned an accounting. If all the money had been spent, I at least had a right to know that I had had an inheritance from my family.

I drove down the sloping street and across the bridge over the Glane, away from the extinct town of Oradour, carrying the images of my mother, of my childhood friend with me as I went. I was also carrying a photograph Léon had given to me taken at his wedding. The old black-and-white image showed the bride and groom in front of the church surrounded by well-wishers. Among the throng was my father. In profile, he could not be made out very well, but it was him, Léon was certain. In the black-and-white blur I could make out only the shape of his angular head, the long slope of his nose, the jut of his chin, the full head of dark wavy hair not unlike my own. He had been perhaps a bit taller than the other men for his head was visible only because it was above the others in the crowd. My mother was probably standing right beside her husband, but, a short woman, she could not be seen. If only I could have asked the others to move aside a little so I could see her. But I could only imagine what she looked like standing there in her best dress with all the well-wishers on that happy, long-ago day.

FONTVIELLE, 1963

11

The light from hundreds of white candles illuminated a grove of evergreen trees lining the altar. The plain wooden cross was in semi-darkness. This was a celebration of birth. The death that was to come, for now, was only a shadow in the background, in the future. The figures at the foot of the altar, carved from the local olive tree—a carpenter, his wife, and infant son surrounded by animals of the field, shepherds with their flocks, as well as royalty from afar— were reflections of the congregation, both the lowly and the high-born, wealthy estate owners and simple peasant people from the area, farmers, grape pickers, artisans.

I sat in the very back of the chapel listening to the soprano choir singing the traditional songs of jubilation for this glorious day on which, it was believed, the Redeemer had come to dwell amongst us. *Gloria in excelsis Deo,* they sang, joyful and triumphant. I had always loved this night above all others, but I felt only loneliness and betrayal, for my Redeemer had not been born to me after all.

I had arrived unnoticed. The faithful had already gathered together and the midnight Mass had already begun when I slipped through the front door of the convent. I thought to wait in my room until the liturgy was over, but I was drawn by the sweet voices of the women who had raised me to love God and to believe in my redemption. I sat in the last row of the chapel hoping that my despair would miraculously fall from me as the scales had fallen from the blind man's eyes at Jesus' touch, but no spiritual wonders came to pass for me that night. I hoped that my doubt was not visible. I hoped that the fires of Oradour-sur-Glane that had consumed my faith did not radiate from me.

When the time came for the worshippers to rise and go forward to receive the Lord that had just been born to them, I remained seated. Perhaps, for the love of those who had raised me to God, I would have gone forward, but they did not even know I was there, so I thought that such hypocrisy was unnecessary.

I sat on the edge of the bed in my orphan room. It was late and I was exhausted. All I wanted to do was sleep, hopeful that my dreams would not unlock any more images of my early childhood stored away deep in my brain. Mother Céline appeared in the doorway.

When I left Oradour I felt as though I didn't love Mother Céline anymore and the loss of love creates a hole that fills quickly with desperation and remorse.

"You must be hungry," she said.

"I am too tired."

"Perhaps a little something on a tray."

"No, really, I couldn't." Tonight I would not allow the mother to bring nourishment for the child, as though I were trying to punish her. She did not insist as had always been her way.

Mother Céline pulled up a chair by the bed and sat down. She was silent, she seemed unsure what to say. She was a woman always in control, but not tonight. Confronted with her sad and worried expression, I could feel all the anger I had accumulated in Oradour falling away. I looked at her concerned and aged face within the halo of her ruff and I loved her again, greatly, perhaps even more than before, my imperfect angel mother. Loving her as I did, I was sorry about what I had to tell her.

"I have been to Oradour."

"I was afraid that might be so."

"I had to go."

"I understand. Christine, we have lied to you all these years. You know this now. The first thing I want to tell you is that, as the head of this community, it was my decision and mine alone not to tell you the truth about your origins. The others, who were, of course, bound by their vow of obedience, had no choice but to do as I told them to do. So the fault is mine and mine alone. I did not tell even my confessor of my decision so certain was I at the time that my actions were correct. I did not see the lies as sin. I rationalized that it was better for you not to know the truth and that was the excuse the devil provided me. I see now, too late, that truth is what God requires of us, and this for good reason since truth makes itself known in the end. But more importantly, lies take too much of value away from us.

"You see, I loved you too much. This, too, is my sin. I loved you more than all the others. I don't know why. I loved the others too. But, since truth is what we are about now, I loved you more. I wanted to protect you. I didn't know how, even when you were older, to tell you of the horrible way in which your parents, your family had died. How can you tell a child, a young girl just on the brink of life, of such a thing, such evil, such pain, without taking away the innocence of childhood, without taking away the joy of life, without taking away, I was so afraid of this, the love of God? It is difficult enough for adults to understand the meaning of such events as occurred in Oradour. And then, you see, you didn't seem to remember anything, anything at all. And so I thought it was God who had washed your mind clean of the terrible things you must have seen, and that it was His plan for you not to know the truth. I got all mixed up. I am the head of this community, and I got all mixed up. I lost my way and I took you and all the others down the road of my deceit. I even consulted with a child psychologist in Aix. He told me it was best that you never know about Oradour. I do not tell you this as an excuse, just as the rationalization that the devil provided for me."

"Mother, I do not blame you. I did at first. I was angry and upset. But no longer."

"You would have every right. Tell me how you found out about Oradour. Was it something I said?"

"No, no, nothing like that. It was just, well, I saw things in my head, just flashes of things, blurry things, like a flash-bulb going off illuminating something for just an instant before it all goes dark again. And dreams I didn't understand.

Of course, we all have dreams we don't understand, and so I didn't pay too much attention over the years. But then, something happened."

"Something happened?"

"When President Kennedy was killed, I was, well, we all were, assigned to the aftermath of the assassination, and of course, I was upset, we were all upset, and then I saw Oswald shot—I mean I was watching the television and I saw him get shot—and I heard the popping sound of the gun when he got shot, and the sound, the popping sound, I knew I had heard this sound before. The popping sound, it was so small really, but I knew what it was and it started a whole chain of memories. I knew I had seen this before, someone being shot, I mean, I had seen before, though I didn't know how that was possible, or where I had seen this, or anything, but I knew it all the same, I just knew it. And then as the days passed I had more flashing images, terrible, and night-mares, and I became more and more, I don't know, agitated and depressed, frightened. I was so filled with anxiety, anxiety was eating at me. I couldn't sleep, I couldn't eat. I didn't understand what was happening to me. I thought I was going crazy. I took a leave of absence from work. I told them there was an illness in the family. I lied, you see, I told them some-one was ill and I had to go home. After I got here, that night, I awoke in the middle of the night and I couldn't get back to sleep. I was so restless, agitated. I wandered about, I walked into the library and I remembered the night I had come here for the first time. When I saw you that night I thought you were an angel. Did I ever tell you? No? You looked like an angel with a halo. You smile, but it's true, you did. I had been afraid until I saw you, and then I wasn't afraid anymore. And you walked me down the room, it was a dormitory then, the library, and you walked me down the long room to my bed, and as we went along you told the other children that I was Christine of Oradour. Do you remember that? No? You said it over and over. 'This is Christine of Oradour,' you said to the others. I had forgotten. But that night of my return, when I went into the library, I could see the way it had been that first night when I came here as a little girl, the room all lined with beds, all the other girls, and you, an angel, calling me Christine of Oradour. You don't remember? I knew I had to find this Oradour. You had told me I was from Limoges, so I thought perhaps Oradour was a section of Limoges, or a suburb, something like that. I had no idea of what I would find. I just thought I had to go there, to see what it was like, to remember something perhaps. I did not know what I would find. But my flashes made me afraid, I think, afraid that something terrible had once happened, something that I had seen. I should have left it all alone. I should never have gone. But it was as though I had no choice. I never imagined I would find a place like Oradour, a place where time just came to a stop one day and everything changed."

"Yes, everything changed. The whole world changed."

"There are names on a stone monument, my mother and father, my grandparents, my two brothers. I had two brothers."

"I know."

"I had a family, a big family. I had a town. I had a best friend. I had a house with a garden. I had a grandfather who was a printer. I had a grandfather who was a bookbinder. Isn't that a wonderful thing to be? I had an uncle who was wounded at Flanders. I had an aunt who was a fine pastry chef. I had . . . "

"You see, that is what I mean. My lies took all that away from you. I should have told you. I should have found the right time, the right way."

"No, you are wrong. You should not have told me. I wish I did not know. I wish I had never found out the truth."

"You are grieving now, as you should have done years ago."

"Yes."

"You could be going forward now, instead you are going backward. You should find a fine young man, you should marry and have a family."

I laughed. "How do you know I don't have a vocation?"

"Because I know you so well. You love the world, you love being part of the world, contributing to its betterment. You have already spent too much of your life in a convent. I was so happy when you went off to Paris, and then New York. I wanted you to learn and to grow, to discover, to meet new people."

"You mean a nice young man."

"And others, too. But yes, a nice young man. What's wrong with that? All mothers want that for their daughters."

"Of course I want that too. I have dreamt of that, having an ordinary family in an ordinary home."

"Yes, I see. Ordinary."

"Oh, I didn't mean it like that. You and the others gave me a fine home."

"But I understand, my dear. Growing up in a convent with nuns is not ordinary, though we tried to make it as ordinary as we could. Most people don't understand that those of us who live in convents are quite ordinary people really. We cry and laugh. We love the pleasures of this world. We have our doubts. We are sinful. We tell lies. We are ordinary humans. But not ordinary in the sense you mean, ordinary parents in an ordinary home. You will have that one day, I am certain of it. But before this can happen you have to come to terms with what you have just learned in Oradour. All I can do is stand by to help you if I can and pray that one day you can forgive me my sin against you."

"What sin? Where is the sin? I don't see sin now. I was angry before, but not now. There is no sin. You loved me. You didn't want me to know about evil. I am glad you lied to me. I am glad for all the time I had when I didn't know what had really happened, when I didn't have such visions of horror in my head. I wish I had never found out the truth."

Of the two lies on which I had been raised, the existence of a kind and loving God who rules the universe was the most difficult to confront. I did not speak of this lie, born not of sin but of a faith made only stronger by this good woman's constant struggle with doubt. I did not tell Mother Céline that her worst fear, the greatest one that had prompted her lies about Oradour, had come to pass, that I no longer believed in God's love. I could not wound her so. I did not want to break my angel mother's heart by telling her that, in my first and only testing, grievous though it was, I had been found weak and wanting. As I looked at the worried woman before me, her face as much creased with concern as wrinkled with age, I hoped that her belief was right and that my denial was wrong. I was startled that a hope of any kind remained but grateful still. For as dreadful as the images of terrible fire and excruciating pain and unimaginable terror, more dreadful still was the contemplation of such human suffering as meaningless and devoid of grace.

PARIS, 1964

12

I was in no shape to face living again in New York, so I went to Paris from the convent. I arranged with *World* to resume my old job in the Paris office without any problem. I'm sure Anatole Osterwald was just as glad to be rid of his exchange student, too soft and unblinking as I was.

My wonderful little apartment seemed like a gift from my father, for I paid the rent out of the inheritance from my family's property, a not inconsiderable sum which had grown over the subsequent years. The money had not been touched but had been held in trust to be distributed to me upon my marriage, to become my dowry if I entered the order, or, if I did not marry or choose the religious life, to be turned over to me upon my thirtieth birthday. It had been determined by the mother superior in Paris that I was not even to be told of the trust before the conditions for distribution had been met for fear that knowledge of my assets would unduly influence my decisions about my path in life. According to the order, a conservative and traditional institution, a young woman on her own, without a husband, without superiors, was not capable of managing money or even contemplating a windfall until she reached age thirty. Only Mother Céline's determination persuaded the convent to sign over the trust without my having fulfilled any of the requisites. I was grateful to receive my money, my father's money, for it set me free. Upon receipt of my account, I relinquished any lingering anger that I had not been told earlier of my inheritance.

The money not only made it possible for me to live on my own, but it also enabled me to leave my job and to pursue my studies in history. I didn't know anything about managing finances, but if I was careful, frugal, I thought that the money would last long enough for me to get my advanced degree and would give me the opportunity to teach and to write of my little town and of my family, to bring them back to life in a way. I wanted to make Oradour, its life and its death, known to the world. I would tell the story of Oradour, and the story of Tulle, and the story of other tragedies infinitesimal within the context of a worldwide war, so they would not be completely forgotten, so they too would be a warning for the future about the horror of war, about how the hatred fortified by war spreads and becomes an insane and irrational lust for blood and revenge. I was determined that my family dead, and my family still living at the convent, and Léon, a historian in his own right, and my dear friend Sophie would be proud of what I would do with the life that had been spared.

"My God, what has happened to you?"

"Happened? Nothing. Nothing has happened."

Sophie pushed her way past me. "Nothing? You look like death dug up. It's the middle of the day, though you'd never know it in here, it's so dark. And you're in your nightclothes. Are you ill? Why didn't you call? Are you ill?"

"No, no, I'm fine, really."

"You don't look fine. You haven't been in class. You don't answer the phone. What has happened, Christine? Tell me at once. You have made me worry. I don't like to worry."

"I'm sorry."

"Say what it is, Christine, so I don't worry."

"I, I've, I am not from Fontvielle, as I told you. Well, that's not right. I am from Fontvielle, but not originally. I only came to Fontvielle when I was six years old."

"What has that got to do with anything?"

"Something happened to me in America. Something happened that made me remember things. I had a memory, a flashback I guess you could say, from my childhood, from my early childhood, before I went to live in Fontvielle. Things have not been the same for me since. I, that is, now, since I returned to France, I have confirmed that memory, the memory is real. And more. I remember more, little by little, day by day. And these new memories are real. My recurring dreams are real."

"My God, Christine, what memories? What do you remember? I don't understand what you are trying to tell me."

"I was born and lived until I was six years old in Oradour-sur-Glane. Do you see? Do you see what I am saying? I am from Oradour."

Sophie squinted her eyes as though someone had shone a light in her face. Her mouth tightened. Her hand came up from her side, the palm outward as though she were warding off a blow. She understood. She had not said a word, but I could see she understood. She knew what had happened. She saw what I was saying. As others recognize the words Auschwitz or Hiroshima or Dresden or Lidice, Sophie recognized the word Oradour.

"Oh my dear, sweet friend. How brave you are. How you have suffered and how very brave you are," Sophie said, and she took me in her arms.

She led me to the sofa and made me sit. She rummaged through my kitchen, found what little was there, and forced the food upon me, an egg, a piece of cheese, a cup of hot chocolate from a packet. I was surprised how good the food tasted.

I told her what I knew of my family's destruction. I told her of the moment I had lost God, of how my life had come apart without Him. Sophie said, "When you thought your family died of illness, you did not blame God. When you found out your family was killed by the hand of man, then you blamed God. It seems to me you have got it the wrong way around."

I couldn't help but smile. Her words sounded so sensible, so simple.

"You know, Christine, this has been the human dilemma since man first walked the earth. If there is an almighty being who made the world, who gave us life, how can that being allow so much evil, so much suffering? Hardly a new question. If there is a definitive answer, I've never heard it. And now, for us, that dilemma is so much worse. The war has changed everything, for everyone, for all time. No one's relationship to man or to God will ever be as it was before. It will be that much harder. We have to begin anew to make sense of life. The paradigms have been altered. We have seen evil as no one before us ever has. There has always been war and atrocity, but never on such a grand and universal scale. Everyone now knows what evil is, what it looks like, how it sounds. We can no longer deny its existence. We know the form evil takes, we know the details. Evil has been visited upon us as never before in history. Before it was only sin. What a benign word that now seems, sin, nothing to the evil that we have seen. Beyond sin. We have the pictures forever in our head. The dead are dead, but we must live with the new knowledge of evil for the rest of our lives. That evil isn't God, Christine, that evil is man. If you told me you were holed up in here never wanting to see a human being again, well, honestly, I'd understand that. But you've barricaded yourself against God. Well, I don't know, I've never been religious really, I don't know what sort of almighty being to believe in, but your reasoning doesn't make a lot of sense to me. God didn't take away our families in a horrible, brutal way, man did."

"*Our* families?"

"I am Jewish, Christine. My family died in Auschwitz. Steffa was the only one who returned to me. I was hidden with a family in a small hill town near Nice. I was a child. I was hidden. But all the rest, my parents, my two brothers, my two other sisters, all the family I had in Hungary, everyone killed. Steffa is all I have left, except for a few relatives I don't know in America. Steffa has seen evil up close, has felt it on her skin, in her mouth, in her nostrils. It has starved her and degraded her and made her mad with terror and grief. She has not told me anything, she cannot speak of it. We all have to live with terrible pictures in our heads, but hers must be the worst of all and they have given her a tenuous hold on her sanity."

"I should have realized. How could I have not understood? I knew we had an affinity, something in common that drew us to one another almost at once. I didn't know it was the terrible pictures in our heads."

"To have lost everyone. How brave you are to even keep on breathing. Do you know how brave you are?"

"You lost everyone. You go on."

"I have Steffa. Perhaps without her I could not. She needs me."

"I need you."

"I need you too. We shall have each other."

"I do not even remember those I lost. Well, my mother, I remember a little of my mother."

"Even if you don't remember with your mind, you remember those you lost with your heart and your genes and your blood. You are everything they were and saw and did. Everything they knew, everything they valued is in you, even if you are not aware of it. Do you understand that?"

"Oh, Sophie, I don't know."

"You will know, just as I know. You have memories of them that you don't even recognize as memories, a feeling from a smell or a sound, a flower, a piece of music, a taste that is familiar somehow. You are what they were, and then you are more because you are you."

"Yes, I do believe that. I felt that way even before I went to Oradour. But now that I know the way they died, the way they must have suffered, every feeling, every memory is tainted by the horror they endured. I sometimes wish I had never found out how they died."

"You will never get over losing them and you will never get over the way they died. But when I am overwhelmed by the terrible death my family suffered, I light up a Gauloise, I take a drink of wine, I make my hands into fists, I dig my nails into my palms, and I force myself to think instead of how I am making them happy and proud, doing what they would have me do, going to school, getting my degree, being with Steffa. That is what I do. You'll find your own way."

Sophie came to stay with me in my apartment. If Monsieur Bernac noticed the new resident, he did not say anything. I was happy to have Sophie with me, to know that she was living in decent surroundings. I loved to pamper her. I loved to cook good meals for her.

We told each other everything we could remember about what had happened to us and to our families during the war, but then we never spoke again of atrocious death by fire or gas or bullet or starvation. We spoke of what we had done that day, what we planned to do tomorrow. We spoke again of movies and plays, music and books, what we would have for dinner, plans for a picnic in the country. We spoke of friends and teachers, movie stars and the latest fashions. We spoke of many, many things, but not of death, only of life, the life we were living now or the future life we planned.

When Steffa came to visit I gave the two of them the double bed in my room and took the daybed in the sitting room where Sophie usually slept. It was wonderful not to be all alone. It was like having sisters again. It was like having God again, doing for others, thinking of others more than of myself. Especially Steffa. When she smiled, when she took pleasure, for even a few minutes, in a meal, in a stroll through a park in the sunshine, in a little gift of bath powder or a bouquet of spring flowers, it was as though faith were mine again. These were moments of joy such as I had known when I beheld the once glorious and beneficent God in the golden monstrance on the altar of the convent.

Sophie said I would find God in other people, that one day I would have a familiar feeling that I would recognize as God and then I would know that He was with me.

One afternoon, as we sat in the Jardin du Luxembourg enjoying the sights and sounds of the spring that had come in spite of everything, Steffa, who never spoke of the past, said, "When I see the daffodils and the tulips, I remember my mother in her garden. I used to help her. She was always happy in her garden." Steffa's memory seemed somehow to be my own, and the sharing was a moment, as Sophie had said there would be, of recognizing God in another person.

Sophie and I were having dinner with some friends in a bistro off the Boulevard St-Michel that was inexpensive and served hearty fare—stews and cassoulets and thick soups—to fill the stomach of ravenous students with not much money to spare. The conversation had turned to movies, a favorite student topic.

"I just saw the new American movie with Gregory Peck," Sophie said. "He's one of my favorites, and it is truly a fine movie. I would even call it a masterpiece."

Ahh, here we go, I thought. I had pretty much given up the fight for French objectivity where American culture was concerned, and so Sophie was usually a lone voice in her defense of the country she admired and longed to visit. French students were, in large measure, condescending toward America and Americans, and almost unanimous in their opinion that American movies were vastly inferior to French films, which were, to them, the best in the world. They would be reluctant to admit that an American movie had artistic merit even if they thought it did.

"What's it called?" Luc asked, an argumentative tone in his voice already.

"*To Kill A Mockingbird*," Sophie answered in the funny way she had with English words.

"Oh, I read about that one," Isabelle said. "It sounds to me like a sentimental apologia for racism in America. It just glosses over the real racist problems that have never been solved."

"That's not true," Sophie countered. "It doesn't gloss over the problems at all. In fact, it meets them head on. It doesn't justify racism, it condemns it absolutely."

"Look at what is happening in America right now," Isabelle persisted. "Race riots and Negro leaders being assassinated, that, oh, what's his name, an odd name, I can't remember. . . ."

"Medgar Evers," Sophie said, and I thought she was going to sigh but she restrained herself.

"That's it, Medgar Evers. And those other three civil rights workers that were murdered. That was terrible."

"But at least people are trying to do something about it. We have plenty of bigotry here in France. Look at what happened during the war. And what did most people do in the face of such persecution? For the most part they did nothing. In fact, it was the French police who conducted the roundups. Not just under Vichy, but in Paris, right here in Paris. The Vichy government ran its own concentration camps. And the French police administered the transit camps and the deportations. And then, of course, there were the Miliciens, Frenchmen who actively aided the Germans. Did you know? Christine and I are studying all about this. So where is the French film masterpiece on France during the war? I've not heard of one. No one has the courage. Everyone is too ashamed to tell the truth. I am waiting for the truth to be told."

This last was meant to incense, and it had succeeded, judging by the stony expressions on the faces of those around the table. I longed to be more like Sophie. She had her strong convictions, and she was never shy about speaking up for what she thought was right. She was always willing to take a stand even if she was alone on her platform. If someone was needed to tell the truth about France during the war, maybe it would be Sophie.

"My God, Sophie," Luc said, ignoring the question of wartime truth, "you can't compare American cinema to European. You've been spending too much time with Christine," he added and everyone looked at me and laughed.

Did Luc and the others have any idea what Sophie had suffered? It seemed not. They must have known she was Jewish. How could it not occur to them what the question of wartime truth meant to her? But then I hadn't added things up properly myself. I hadn't imagined what Sophie had gone through until she finally told me about her childhood during the war. I thought to say something to the others, but I hesitated. Perhaps I had no right to speak for Sophie about the French betrayal of her family. But I didn't have to speak because, to my surprise, for she was always reticent on the subject, Sophie spoke for herself.

"I also want you to know," she began, "that I survived the war because there were good people who protected me. Without such fine French people, many more would have died."

"Who were they, Sophie, the ones who helped you?" David asked.

"Well, my father had the sense to make the family separate. I had a baby brother who needed to remain with my mother, so I was put in the care of my Aunt Ruthie. She must have been so scared to be on her own at such a time, she was only nineteen after all, and with responsibility for the welfare of a small child. We went on the run, toward the South. We never stayed more than a few days in any one place. I remember one night we slept in a field, and I cried and cried because it was so damp and cold. I don't know exactly how she managed this, and my memory of this time is not exact, I was so young, but Aunt Ruthie left me with a family in a small town not far from Nice. I was so scared at first, being left with strangers. But the people were very kind to me.

They had children of their own for me to play with and, this stands out in my mind, there was plenty to eat. They grew their own vegetables and I would help in the garden. They even took me to church with them, which was very strange to me. Not scary, but strange. I don't know what they told their friends and neighbors about me. I don't know if everyone knew that I was Jewish. If they did, no one seemed to care. There was no attempt to hide me away. Everyone in the town just seemed to accept my presence."

"What happened to your Aunt Ruthie?" David asked.

"She went on to Marseilles where she found work in a restaurant. Her employer must have known she was a Jew for the only papers she had were marked with a big red "J." But he employed her anyway and put her to work in the kitchen where she was out of sight. And he let her sleep in a room at the back of the restaurant. This was very dangerous, for he could have been shot if he was caught harboring a Jew, but he did it anyway. Her employer and her fellow workers never betrayed her. So you see, running from the Germans and the French police and the Miliciens, we also found good French people who made it possible for us to survive."

"Did you ever see Ruthie again?" Luc wanted to know.

"Oh, yes. At the end of the Occupation, Aunt Ruthie came for me and we returned to Paris. I was so excited because I thought we were going home and that my parents and the rest of my family would be waiting for us. But by then, of course, there were strangers living in our apartment as well as in the apartment where Aunt Ruthie's family used to live. I don't know what happened to our furniture, all the possessions we had to leave behind. None of the neighbors had seen my parents and the concierge refused to talk to us. Aunt Ruthie rented us a small room and she found work in a nearby garment factory. She worked at night, so she put me to bed before she left. I was scared, being all alone at night, but I tried to be brave for Aunt Ruthie."

"And the rest of your family?" Isabelle asked timidly, as though afraid of the answer.

"Well, shortly after our return, the trips to the Gare de l'Est began. At that time trains were arriving bringing concentration camp survivors back from the East. So that is where we went to search for our family, to the gare. As soon as a train arrived, Aunt Ruthie would grab my hand and we'd run frantically from person to person as the passengers detrained. She'd thrust the few family pictures she had saved into the faces of the survivors. She'd plead with these poor people to look at her tattered old photographs. 'Please,' she'd beg, 'have you seen this woman? This man? This child?' 'I have seen some children,' one man told her, 'but they were put on a train to Russia and so I don't know what happened to them.' A gaunt woman said, 'Don't hope, your heart will only be broken. Most everyone was killed, and children, no, no, they didn't stand a chance.' But Aunt Ruthie wouldn't give up. We went back to the gare over and over and over. She'd beg and weep and run from person to person forcing as many as possible to look at her photographs. At first I was embarrassed when she accosted people, but soon enough I was doing as she did, running, tugging on people's arms, begging for information. We never saw anyone from our family alight from a train from the East."

"Oh, God," Isabelle said, "I am so sorry, Sophie."

"But two years later, with the help of the Red Cross, we found my sister Steffa in a hospital just north of Paris. The doctors had managed to bring her starved body back to health. She had survived because she had been young and strong on her arrival at Auschwitz and she had been put to work sorting the belongings of those sent to the gas chambers. Difficult work, but not the kind that wore you to death. Steffa told us that everyone else in the family had died, but Aunt Ruthie would not accept this. After all, everyone had separated. How could Steffa know that everyone had been deported? Surely some had escaped, as Aunt Ruthie and I had. 'Did you see the others in the camp?' Aunt Ruthie demanded. 'Did you see them die?' Steffa had not seen anyone except our sister Klara, who had been captured with her in Lyon and had died of typhus in the camp. And so Aunt Ruthie, her hope fueled by Steffa's vagueness, continued to search. Eventually she found her way to the organization run by Serge Klarsfeld, the expert on the fate of the Jews from France, where it was confirmed and documented, down to the dates of deportation and death, that everyone else in our family was dead. Everyone but Aunt Ruthie's mother, who was not listed on the roster of the doomed. Aunt Ruthie never gave up looking for her, hoping. Once she even went to Marseilles because she had read in the newspaper that a ship from Russia loaded with camp survivors was due to arrive there. But her mother was not among them. Aunt Ruthie died of pneumonia. She was only thirty-two years old. I think she just gave up. All the loss was too much for her in the end. I was eighteen when she died, and then it was just me and Steffa."

There was silence around the table. I could see that our garrulous friends did not know what to say in response to Sophie's portion of France's wartime truth.

"I could go for another beer," Sophie said, breaking the awkward moment. "Anyone else?"

We all nodded.

"On me," David said. "The beers are on me."

Despite all that had happened, Sophie believed that the good would win out if we just kept plugging away. When I thought of my mother and father, of all those who had been killed in Oradour, of all those who had perished during the war, I would be overcome by doubt, but Sophie always brought me round. If she ever faltered, I never saw it happen. I only saw tears in her eyes the once, when she told me about her Aunt Ruthie running frantically and in vain from person to person at the Gare de l'Est.

The worst loss of all is the loss of hope. But Sophie never lost hope, and that is her grace and her strength and her beauty. My hope used to be in God. Now it is in Sophie. When she told me that I would find God in other people, I don't think she realized that she was talking about herself.

Sophie and I were gathering herbs along the riverbank to flavor our meals during the coming week. Steffa was stretched out on a blanket taking the sun. Luc and David had driven us to Île-de-France just north of Paris for a Sunday in the country, and we had chosen to stop at the quiet village of Moret-sur-Loing where we had picnicked alongside the placid river that flows through the town. Now Luc was trying his luck with his fishing pole, and David, ever the bookworm, was reading a novel. As I watched Sophie that day, I thought she might have feelings for David. And I watched him, too, for any sign that he might be drawn to her as well. I had come to no conclusion. I wanted all the good things of life for Sophie, even as I did for myself, including a fine man to love and to be loved by in return.

The sky was blue, not the intense blue of Provence, but a gentler, iridescent blue that made me feel at ease. There were no clouds and so we had the full warmth of the summer sun upon us, but the river provided a kindness—a slight and cooling breeze. The branches of the willow trees hung low along the banks of the Loing, the air was filled with the earthy smell of nearby farms and forests.

I bent to pick another bunch of parsley, and when I straightened, Sophie caught my eye and smiled. She pointed in the direction of a small barge with two men polling. Or perhaps she was pointing beyond them at the dome of the Sacré-Coeur visible in the distance, the air was that clear. I heard a yelp, and I looked over at Luc, who had just caught his first fish of the day. He held up his conquest for me to admire, and he looked very pleased with himself, for an admirable river pike it was. Then he quickly freed the fish from the hook and threw it back into the river. I am very partial to fish as a meal, but I felt strangely happy that he had thrown this one back. I turned toward Sophie, who was standing with her eyes closed, her face upturned toward the sun. Whenever I saw Sophie in a rare quiet attitude, I would wonder, as I did now, if she was thinking of her lost family.

I brought the herbs up to my face to smell the goodness of the chervil and the sorrel and the parsley. A breeze off the river where Luc's liberated fish was going about his life passed over me, and the summoning sound of a church bell drew my attention to the aged stone buildings of the town on the other side of the river. Suddenly I was overcome with a weakness, a pleasant light-headedness. I had never been to this place before, yet everything seemed familiar. A memory had just occurred that told me I carried my family within me, what they had seen and felt and heard and tasted and smelled, what they had known and what they had loved. I was all that my family had been and then I was more because I was me, just as Sophie had said. And Sophie, too, was all that her family had been, but she was more, more, more. She was a person I loved. She was a friend who kept me on the straight and narrow, as they say in America, on the path going forward, taking my family with me as I made my way.

ORADOUR, 1944

13

The woman in the flowered dress is standing in her back doorway surveying her garden. She is choosing the flowers she will use in an arrangement for the church altar bouquet. She is smiling. The garden has done well this year, plenty of sunshine, just enough rain. She shields her eyes and looks up at the sky. Not a cloud as far as her eye can see. The good weather will hold, she thinks. Tomorrow will be as sunny and warm as today, a fine day for her daughter's First Holy Communion. She decides to wait until late afternoon to pick the flowers, that they may be at their best for the ceremony.

She steps back into the kitchen. She stirs a saucepan on the stove with a wooden spoon. Then she brings the spoon to her mouth, tastes, and smiles with satisfaction. She sits down at the table and smiles at her daughter Christine who is finishing her lunch. There is a pile of green beans on the table and she starts to cut them into a pot.

"Stop that, you toad," her daughter says to her brother.

"Stop both of you and finish your lunch. This is going to be a busy afternoon. There is no time for foolishness," the woman scolds. She knows her four-year-old son, Jean-Claude, is probably kicking his sister under the table. The baby, Théo, is in the high chair, playing with his lunch more than eating it. Mashed green peas are all over his face and hands. His sister makes a face at him, and the baby giggles and throws his hands up into the air with glee. His spoon clatters to the stone floor.

The woman's husband appears in the kitchen doorway. The woman walks to him, they exchange words. The man nods his head and leaves, the woman returns to the kitchen table.

"Christine, there is a package Papa wants you to take to Père Chapelle," the woman says to the little girl. "Classes are starting a half hour later this afternoon because of the medical exams, so you have time before school. If no one is at the rectory, just leave the package by the back door. He'll know what it is. Now go along, and take a plum, one for Colette."

"Yes, Maman."

"And don't run off with Colette. No going into the woods. Not today."

"The woods?" the little girl says, cocking her head.

"I know you two play in the woods. You'll lose track of the time and I can't have that today. Right after class is rehearsal, and then I need you to help me make a bouquet of flowers for the altar. Oh dear, I wanted you to pick some herbs for me as well. Never mind, there won't be enough time. I'll do it later. The salve for Abbé Chapelle is more important."

"Yes, Maman."

"Remember what I said about the woods. You've already made your confession, there is not time for another," the woman says with a laugh and kisses her daughter good-bye. The woman wonders what the little girl, so innocent, so guileless, had to tell the priest in the confessional. Such little sins, she thinks. Not even sins really, just the normal behavior of a child.

The woman quickly finishes cutting the beans into the pot. She clears the table, washes the lunch dishes. Then she puts Théo and Jean-Claude down for an afternoon nap, the baby already half asleep, the little boy complaining all the way upstairs that he isn't tired.

She returns quickly to the kitchen and assembles all the ingredients for the almond cake she is to make on the pine table worn smooth by its service to her family. Flour, butter, eggs, sugar, chopped almonds, vanilla. She can almost taste the finished product, when all these ingredients are blended together as her mother taught her when she was a little girl, a splendid dessert for the family party after the First Communion. She used to make this cake for all special family events, but since the war she has had to be more frugal with the sugar and the flour, knowing that when she runs out there will not be more. But tomorrow is such a special day she has decided to be profligate, optimistic that, with the Germans on the run, she will soon be able to make all the cakes she wants, even when there is no special occasion.

The woman has just begun to sift the flour when her husband appears again in the kitchen doorway.

"Something strange is happening," he says.

"Strange?"

"Yes, well, there are soldiers."

"Soldiers?"

"German soldiers."

"Dear Lord. What do they want?"

"They say we must come with them. To the square. For an identity check."

"They've never done this before. Do they want me to come?"

"Everyone. They want everyone."

"The children are asleep."

"You'll have to wake them. I'll get the papers and the pram. The soldiers have made the people from the country-side come to town as well. There is quite a crowd. I've never seen anything like it."

"You'd think they would have better things to do," the woman says. Now I'm not going to get the cake made, she thinks with regret. I'll have to make it tonight. How annoying this is. Why on earth are the Germans wasting time with people in a small village?

She goes upstairs to get her children. Jean-Claude, still awake and restless, is happy to be ordered from his bed. Théo is already sound asleep and is fussy at being disturbed. "Hurry, Jean-Claude, we must go to the town square. Papa is waiting."

"Why?"

"I'm not sure, Sweetheart. Papa will tell you."

When the woman steps out of her front door she is astounded by the number of people in the street, farmers, mothers with babies, children running about, playing hide-

and-seek between the women's legs, kicking up the dirt in the road. She brushes the skirt of her dress, she tries to straighten her hair, but the wayward strands refuse to stay put. She had not thought to be seen today by friends and neighbors. Her husband is waiting with the pram. He smiles encouragingly and gently brushes a smudge of flour from her cheek. The woman puts Théo down on his stomach and, thankfully, he goes back to sleep. She runs back in the house to fetch a bottle of juice for the baby and some biscuits for Jean-Claude. Lord knows how long this foolishness is going to take.

The crowd moves en masse up the street flanked by soldiers carrying guns. The sight of armed soldiers, something she has never seen before, unnerves the woman. But everyone is calm and she is reassured.

"This is very strange," a farmer she does not know says out loud to no one in particular. "I don't like this business, not at all. They must be looking for something, though God knows what."

"Are there Maquisards hiding here?" another asks.

"Of course not," someone answers indignantly.

"How can we be sure?"

"Even if there are, it's a little late now. The Germans have already lost the war, or maybe they don't know that yet."

"There have been Maquisards in Oradour-sur-Vayres. Maybe that's where they think they are, stupid Boches."

"Shut up, they might hear you. Don't cause any trouble. They'll soon be gone if we just do as we're told."

The crowd of men and women and children reaches the town square, where there is another crowd of people waiting.

The mayor is talking with a German officer. The mayor is shaking his head, the expression on his face is very serious. He does not seem to like what the German officer is saying to him. The woman begins to feel uneasy again. She sees a group of schoolchildren across the square with Mademoiselle Bardet, her daughter's teacher. Christine is not with them.

"Claude," she whispers to her husband. "I don't see Christine anywhere."

"Don't worry about her. She'll turn up."

"Maybe she's gone to the woods. I told her not to, but she may have gone anyway."

"Let her be in the woods then. What does it matter? They'll not miss one little girl. In any case, I have her papers."

The woman knows her husband is trying to reassure her, but when she looks in his face she can see he is beginning to worry about the German soldiers and what they want. She is very hot now, the sky is cloudless and the sun is strong. Jean-Claude is getting cranky. "Maman, let's go home," he pleads. "I'm thirsty. I want to go home." "Soon, Darling, soon." She wipes his damp forehead with her handkerchief, she pushes strands of hair wet with perspiration from his flushed face. They have no right to make the children stand here under the hot sun, she thinks with anger. To what purpose?

Now the mayor is talking to Monsieur Depierrefiche, the town crier, who suddenly takes up his drum and starts off, away from the square, just as the black Citroën belonging to the town's young doctor arrives at the end of the main street. The doctor gets out of his car, walks to the mayor, his father, and the German officer. There is more serious discussion. Then orders are given to the crowd in French. The men are to sit on the ground in rows facing the buildings lining the square, while the women and the children are to assemble in the church.

The woman looks at her husband for reassurance. He smiles at her but there is a certain lack of conviction in his face. He nods his head as though to say, do as they order, everything will be alright. "Don't worry about Christine. She's better off in the woods," he whispers.

The woman watches as her husband walks away to join the other men seated on the ground. She sees Abbé Chapelle. Poor man, she thinks. He is old and in pain. How hard this must be for him. He probably didn't have a chance to try the new salve.

The woman moves off down the hill toward the church holding Jean-Claude by the hand, pushing the baby in the pram. It feels as though she is not moving under her own steam but that the momentum of the huge crowd is carrying her along. The sound of the children's wooden clogs on the pavement sounds like thunder in her ears, there are so many of them. She looks back over her shoulder at the men of her town hunched on the ground and she is filled with fear at the sight. She knows this is not an identity check. This is something else, but she doesn't know what. Maybe the rumors about the kidnapping of a German officer are true. Dear God, maybe they think he is being hidden in this town. Well, they'll find soon enough that he is not here and that will be the end of it, she says to herself in a desperate effort to keep her fear in check. She is also worried that Christine will arrive at the school to find everyone gone. She'll go home to an empty house and will be afraid. For once the woman hopes that her daughter has been very naughty, that she has run off to the woods with Colette and has lost track of time.

The great mass of women and children arrives at the church and everyone is motioned inside by the soldiers gesturing with their rifles. At least it is cool in here, the woman thinks. Théo is awake and fussy. She tries to give him the bottle but he pushes it away. She knows he needs to be changed, but in her haste she has forgotten to bring a clean diaper.

"Isn't this an awful thing?" she hears a woman say behind her. She turns to see a mother struggling to quiet her little girl. "I have to go to the bathroom, Maman," her child pleads. The young mother looks at the woman and says, "What am I to do? Should I ask if I can take her to a bathroom, or outside at least?" The woman is at a loss. She doesn't know what advice to give. She would be afraid to approach one of the armed soldiers. They are very young but the rifles make them look so threatening.

Suddenly the doors to the church that had been closed by the soldiers are flung open. Two soldiers move down the main aisle carrying a large box which they place on the floor at the center of the church. There is a loud popping sound outside and the soldiers bend over and put lighters to white cords hanging from the box. Immediately thick, black smoke begins pouring out and quickly spreads.

Within seconds there is panic. Women are screaming, children are weeping. The smoke is suffocating. The woman in the flowered dress grabs her baby from the pram, she seizes her little boy's hand, and she starts to run, instinctively trying to escape from the smoke.

"God save us," the woman cries as she tries to protect her baby with her skirt, wrapping his head in yellow flowers and green leaves as though she can keep him safe within the garden of her dress.

"Maman, Maman," Jean-Claude cries.

"Sweet, holy Jesus," the woman cries.

"Maman, Maman," Jean-Claude cries.

Soldiers move into the church with armloads of wood and kindling to which they set fire. Flames rise and spread rapidly.

With one arm wrapped about her baby, the woman drops to her knees and puts her other arm about the shoulders of her little boy. She holds her children against the breasts that nourished them in infancy. She turns toward the wall of the church so her children cannot see the desperate sight of people burning, people dying. *Sancta Maria, mère de Dieu, mère de Dieu . . .*

She hears the staccato sound of machine guns, the exploding sound of grenades. She has never heard these sounds before but she knows what they are. Flames are all about her now, coming closer, growling as they feed on the wooden chairs and the kindling the soldiers have brought as an offering, hissing and snarling as they consume everything in their path. *Sed libera nos a malo,* she prays, entreating God to deliver her and her babies from this evil being visited upon them. There is no individual sound of her terror. Her pleas and cries are subsumed within the tremendous collective moan of suffering and horror. There is nowhere to run. She is trapped by God's thick stone walls. She pushes her children to the hard floor and winds herself around them in an attempt to absorb all the hellfire within herself. *Dust thou art, dust thou art.* She learned this lesson as a child, reminded each year when the priest smudged the ash on her forehead. The ash, the words had no meaning for her then, young, so far from death. Still, she did not forget the lesson, and she surrenders herself, bone and skin and muscle and sinew, offers her body, combustible, unsustainable, up for immolation. *Unto dust thou shalt return, unto dust thou shalt return,* a warning becomes a promise and a hope that the ash she will become might extinguish the fire before it can pass through her and reach her children. Her offering is not accepted. A barrage of machine gun fire rakes across the kneeling woman wrapped around her children, making of them a oneness in death as they had been in life. *Sed libera nos a malo, a malo, a malo* . . .

Before the church bells have melted and the arching has collapsed, before the conflagration has spread throughout, consuming everything within the consecrated walls, the pain and the terror for the woman in the dress with the yellow flowers and the little green leaves, spared a death by fire, is over.

PARIS, 1964

14

"Hi, hello, is this Christine?"

"Yes, this is Christine Lenoir. Who is this, please?"

"This is Christine Lenoir of Paris, France? The one, the only?"

"Brian Malloy, is that you?"

"Yup, it's me."

"The man of science and medicine? The one, the only?"

"Yes, the formerly."

"What do you mean, formerly?"

"Well, I've given World, Inc., the heave-ho."

"The heave-ho?"

"Sorry. American slang. I quit the magazine. Couldn't stand it anymore."

"Wow! What are you doing now?"

"Look, I'll tell you all about it. When can I see you?"

"See me? Where are you?"

"Right here in Paris. You made me wonder what I'd been missing all these years. No one should reach my age without having seen Paris."

"Come at once. Take the metro to École Militaire."

"Hold it right there. I'm just a stupid tourist from the States and my high school French is definitly not making it. I've no idea about the metro. I just got here."

"Then take a cab. I live at 18, avenue de la Motte Picquet."

"Wait. Hold on. I've got to write this down."

I spelled out my address for him and told him to just show it to the cab driver. "Get over here right away. I can't wait to see you. Oh, and when you get here, it's the top floor on the right, and ring the bottom buzzer. The apartment is, well, never mind, you'll see when you get here. Hurry."

I was excited at the prospect of seeing the American man who had been so kind to me during a difficult time. I could see his open Irish-American face, his kind eyes, his warm smile as I ran about picking up the accumulated debris that Sophie and I had managed to scatter about our small apartment. Then I tried to make something of myself. I had planned to spend the day studying, so I hadn't even combed my hair. I wanted to be attractive for Brian, not just cleaned and combed, but alluring, which I really didn't know how to manage, especially on such short notice.

I wasn't surprised that Brian had left *World*. He didn't have that cutthroat, aggressive personality necessary for a good journalist any more than I did. He was soft-spoken and had a gentle wit that his coworkers didn't seem to understand.

He looked too large for my little sitting room. He was, like so many Americans, tall and broad, and my small room made him look even bigger.

"I am so happy to see you. How did you find me?"

"I still have my *World* ID card, so I just flashed it at your office and flirted shamelessly with the woman at the front desk, and voilà, here I am."

"I don't even work there anymore."

"You don't? The woman never said anything. What happened?"

"Oh, don't worry, I'm glad to be gone. I'm much happier now. I hope you are too."

We sat and caught up with each other's lives. Brian was enrolled in a master's program in biology at Boston University starting in the fall. "There is such a shortage of science teachers in the public schools," he told me, "so I thought I'd do my bit for the younger generation. Besides, I think I'll be good at it."

"I'm glad. You'll be great." I told Brian all about my own plans and he looked pleased.

"You know, I was really mad at you when you left New York without saying good-bye. I know, there was an illness in your family, but then I never heard from you again."

"I'm sorry about that. My whole life has been in turmoil since I returned. I'll explain it all to you, but not right now. It's too long and involved and Sophie'll be home any minute."

"Sophie?"

"She's my roommate. We met at the Sorbonne. You'll just love her. She's a lot of fun."

When Brian left me that afternoon, he hesitated at the door. I was suddenly nervous. He leaned toward me and I thought he was going to kiss me. And he did, softly on both my cheeks.

"Isn't that how the French do it?"

"Exactly how the French do it," I said.

He turned and opened the gate to the little lift that ran up and down the center of the building, a lift not made for a man his size. I felt disappointed. I couldn't believe it, but I was actually disappointed. I had wanted him to kiss me, really kiss me, and I was afraid he did not like me in the way I suddenly wanted him to. Don't be stupid, I told myself, this is no time for you to get involved with anyone. Your life is too hectic, and besides, he's only here for a short time and then you'll probably never see him again.

I wanted to show Brian around the city I loved, and we had made a lot of plans for things to do together during the next few weeks. But when he was squeezed inside the lift and before he closed the gate, I said, "Come tomorrow night for dinner." I didn't want to wait until the weekend before seeing him again.

"You sure? I know how busy you are. Don't want to interfere with your life too much."

But I wanted him to interfere with my life. "No, really, it's fine. Tomorrow at 7:00."

"Okay, if you say so. Then I'll take you out for a grand dinner at a fancy restaurant, any one you name. Let's see what those Michelin stars are all about. After all, I still owe you an expensive dinner. Remember?"

"Indeed, you do. I remember very well."

"Okay, then see you tomorrow."

"À demain."

"Hey, I even know what that means. À demain, Christine."

"No, thanks," Sophie said, when I invited her to have dinner with me and Brian. "I have other plans."

"You do not."

"Well, then I'll make some. I'm going to leave you alone with your American friend. You must have a lot to talk about."

"That's not necessary, Sophie, really. Stay," I said. I was being disingenuous. I didn't really want her to stay.

"Nope. The apartment is all yours. And have a good time. Maybe this is the one, you never know. Maybe you'll fall madly in love."

"Sophie, please, he's American. My life is here. I can't fall in love with an American." But then I thought perhaps I could.

"The chicken was delicious. And you told me you weren't a gourmet cook."

"That was a very plain dish."

"Didn't taste plain to me."

"The only hard part is the kitchen, it's so small. Not much like kitchens in America. And the stove is ancient. But there's nothing much to the dish. White wine and garlic and tomatoes and mushrooms, that's what we use a lot of where I come from. And olives. We use a lot of olives and olive oil. Just throw it all together. That's how you make the best dishes in Provence, throw a lot of things in a pot and voilá."

"Tell me about the place you come from."

"Oh, well, the place I come from. Let's see. Near Aix-en-Provence, in the south of France. I grew up in a big old house in the countryside." I failed to mention that the big old house was a convent. "It is very beautiful, where I come from, hills and vineyards, orange and olive groves, cypress trees. I love the cypress. They seem like old friends. How silly that sounds. The colors are wonderful, and the sky is so bright sometimes it hurts your eyes. The landscape, all year round, well, it is very beautiful, always flowers and the scent of oranges and olives and wild herbs all mixed up together."

"I'd love to see it sometime."

"Yes, you must. I'd love to show it to you sometime."

"Christine, not to change the subject, but you told me your life was in turmoil. Is everything alright now?"

"Yes, yes, so much better now."

"Will you tell me about it?"

"Yes, but not right now. It has been such a lovely evening. Let's not spoil it."

"Sounds serious. I don't want to pry. Whenever you are ready. I'm a good listener, you know."

"Yes, I know that. I remember."

That evening Brian and I became lovers. I was getting myself in over my head, but for the moment I didn't care. I knew that I was not acting just out of bodily need, for in what I felt for him I recognized the love I had known throughout my life. I recognized the feel of love from out of the past, from across the years, my memory jogged by the man whose arms were around me.

I recognized the love I had felt as I listened from my bed, when I was a little girl, before sleep came to me, as Mother Céline played the piano in the parlor, the beautiful Chopin preludes and the Debussy *Clair de Lune* and the Beethoven sonatas that were her favorites, and so were mine.

I recognized the love I had felt as I sat in the convent garden under the bright Provençal sky gossiping with my sisters, laughing and whispering and teasing, when our curiosity about the world outside our insulated existence was limitless, and we were so eager for the future in that world to begin.

I recognized the love I had felt when everyone in the family worked together in the orchards and the groves, picking the oranges from the trees, at other times the olives and the figs, each in their season, gathering in the wild herbs that grew in abundance all on their own, and the tomatoes and melons and vegetables that had required our labor to produce; then making these gifts of the land that God had given, again all of us together, into wonderful foods for us to eat and to share with our neighbors, foods fresh from the soil or preserved as jams and conserves and oils and bouquets garnis.

I recognized the love I had felt when I knelt at the altar rail to receive the Lord as my personal redeemer, or when, on the special holy days, I beheld the Lord of Lords displayed in splendor within the golden monstrance, the love radiating like the sun, the warmth penetrating my soul.

And I recognized the love that I had felt when I was a little girl as it came to me across a wooden table in a small, white-tiled kitchen from the woman in the flowered dress, the woman dark and plump, the woman with a warm and pretty smile who was talking to me and smiling as she cut green beans into a pot. The feeling between the mother and the little girl I had been was so strong, and I recognized in it the love I had for the man lying next to me.

If Brian were to be a part of my life, I would have to tell him about the woman in the flowered dress, the full story of my mother and of myself, with all that that telling would imply. I would have to tell him of my origins, that I was, as Mother Céline had called me so many years ago, Christine of Oradour.

But as it was, I had to assume that this relationship was temporary, for Brian would soon return to his life in America, and so telling him my life story would never be necessary. I would put him off if he asked me again about what had made me leave New York so abruptly. For the moment I did not want to think about past pain, and I did not want to think of the future when Brian would be gone.

If God were in other people as Sophie had said, He was surely in the man from America who would teach young students about the wonders of our physical world and who had reminded me of all the love I been vouchsafed throughout my life.

ORADOUR, 1944

15

The day is perfect. The clouds have left the sky to the sun and so the world, as far as the eye can see, is full of light, just as the woman had predicted. There is a profusion of flowers on the altar, from gardens all over the town and the countryside. Abbé Chapelle, in his finest vestments of white and gold, looks somehow younger today, standing straight and tall for this special occasion, waiting at the foot of the altar for the first communicants.

The processional music begins. The congregation rises and turns toward the back of the church, expectant. They are coming now. The girls are first, walking two by two. There she is, there is little Christine, walking with Marie Tavernier. And just behind is Colette Orrefort, Christine's best friend. The woman smiles. She has never seen Christine, or any of the children, for she knows them all, look so serious. Christine's dress and lace veil, finished only a few days ago, is beautiful, she thinks, allowing herself a moment of pride. She tries to catch Christine's eye as she passes, but the little girl is doing as she was told, looking straight ahead, her hands pressed together.

The woman looks down at the baby in her lap. Théo is sleeping soundly, thank heaven. And Jean-Claude is on his best behavior. Her husband, Claude, had a talk with him before they left for church, and he must have made an impression on the little boy, for he has hardly made a peep. She glances over at her husband. He is a fine father, she thinks, firm but never harsh. She is certain that he said the right things to Jean-Claude, but she wouldn't be surprised if he used a little bribery as well, for as a father his heart is soft.

The boys are coming down the aisle. She hardly recognizes her nephew Marcel for she has never seen him this clean and with his unruly hair newly trimmed and plastered in place. She swallows a laugh. She looks across the aisle at Denise Bardet, and they exchange smiles. Christine is lucky to have such a fine teacher.

The church is full of proud parents, beaming relatives. What a milestone, the woman thinks. Next will come the confirmation and someday a wedding. She is distracted as she tries to envision the wedding dress she will make for her daughter. When she comes back to the moment at hand, the children are all seated in the front rows, girls on the right, boys on the left. She looks for Christine, but she cannot see her for she is hidden by the heads of the taller girls.

Père Chapelle bows in front of the stone altar. "In Nomine Patris, et Filii et Spiritus Sancti," he intones. "Amen," the congregation responds. The Mass has begun.

Sometimes the Mass seems long to her, but not today. It is no time at all before the priest is holding up the host and saying, "Hoc est enim corpus meum," transforming the bread into the body of Christ.

The children go forward to receive the Blessed Lord. She sees Christine kneeling in front of the old priest. "Corpus Domini nostri Jesu Christi custodiat animam tuam in vitam aeternam," he says, as he holds the host that will be hers. "Amen," the child answers. Though her mother cannot hear the whispered word, she knows it has been spoken and that Christine is holding her tongue ready for the body of Christ. "In vitam aeternam, vitam aeternam," the woman whispers, confident that her child is well on the path to life everlasting.

She feels very peaceful. She knows that the Lord Jesus will be with her little girl, within her always as He is today. She knows that no matter how hard the road ahead will sometimes be, He will guide her.

Père Chapelle is praying the Pater Noster with the congregation. Théo is beginning to fuss, Jean-Claude to squirm. Never mind. The Mass is almost at an end, and the little boys have been very good. Jean-Claude will surely receive whatever bribe his father had offered, and Théo will be given a special treat as well.

"Sed libera nos a malo, Amen," all the voices pray together the ending of the Pater Noster. "Sed libera nos a malo," the woman repeats to herself, an extra plea for her family and her friends and her townspeople and the war-torn world to be delivered from evil.

Huddled in a hole in the ground, a little girl hears a great sound such as she has never heard before. She does not know what the sound could be. She does not know that it is a cry of human anguish which contains the voices of her mother and her brothers, which contains the words her mother is praying over and over, *sed libera nos a malo, sed libera nos a malo.*

The day the woman has imagined, the day she has anticipated with such joy, disintegrates in a burst of machine gun fire. That day will never come to pass. But the little girl is safe, and her mother knows this, her consolation as she dies that by God's mercy her little girl is safe from the evil that has engulfed the town of Oradour, safe within her hiding place in the woods. *Sed libera nos a malo, libera nos, libera nos, a malo, a malo, a malo . . .*

AMERICA, 1972

16

Brian and I were married in the chapel of the convent at Fontvielle. Only the nuns, three of the orphan girls with whom I had grown up, Sophie and Steffa, and Brian's parents were in attendance. I wore a simple white dress trimmed with lace made for me by Mother Marguerite, the veil of lace Mother Céline had worn at the ceremony when she entered the order as a novice. I carried a bouquet of wildflowers gathered from the local landscape for me by my mothers. The chorus of female voices I had listened to since I was a child sang during the nuptial mass. No bride from a wealthy, aristocratic family could have had a more beautiful ceremony.

Later we shared sandwiches and cake and champagne in the library where I had once slept with the other orphan girls. Mother Céline played the piano, old songs she remembered from when she was a young girl before she joined the order. It was a joyful party.

Brian had returned to America, but he came back over his spring holiday and asked me to marry him. Before I would accept, he had to know about everything that made me the person I am, and so I finally told him about my life, about Oradour and my loss of faith. He was insistent that I make the choice between the tragedy of my past and a future with him. By temperament a gentle and abiding man, he was insistent. By temperament a cautious woman, I was grateful for his fortitude and his perseverance, and, in the end, I accepted the life he offered me. We both understood that the choice could not be exclusive, that the past would accompany me into the future. Brian said he accepted the implications.

The simple wedding in Fontvielle seemed sufficient to sanctify our union, but for Brian's parents we repeated our vows at their home in Massachusetts. We could not deny them. This was not the small and intimate affair I would have wished. The guests filled the church and were served a sumptuous dinner under a tent festooned with flowers and ribbons and candles on the lawn of the Malloy house. The champagne flowed and the band played late into the night. My hand-sewn dress didn't seem quite up to the grandeur of the event, but Brian's mother praised the workmanship and the antique lace and the simple elegance of my bridal attire to one and all, which was very sweet of her. "How many brides have a dress sewn especially for them by French nuns, I should like to know?" she said more than once.

Brian and I live in Boston with our three children. Our daughter, Mary Katherine, is six years old. Our twins, a boy, Devon, and a girl, Bridget, are almost two. I would not give French family names to my children, names that belonged to people who suffered an unspeakable fate. Brian suggested middle names to commemorate my family but I said no. My children were not to be tainted by atrocity. What I will tell them about their maternal ancestors, I do not know. When they are older, will I take them to Oradour? Will I tell them about what happened there? I cannot say. After all, I sometimes wish no one had told me. I sometimes wish that my mind could be swept clean of the pictures of fire and horrific death. How could I ever allow such images into the minds of my children?

Léon Tavernier died not long after Brian and I were married. I saw him one last time. After the wedding in Fontvielle I went with Brian to Oradour. I hoped the visit would help him understand the burdens that I would always carry in case I should ever stagger under the weight of them. In my absence, Léon had grown old and frail and he made me afraid. He was happy to learn of my marriage and to know that I was turning away from death and toward a new life. I shall always be grateful to him, my own personal historian, for the gaps in my life he was able to fill. He gave me images from the life of my family that help to offset the images of death.

Brian has his Ph.D. in biology and he is now teaching at a Boston high school as well as some courses at Boston University. I did freelance work while he finished his studies, now he supports me while I balance motherhood with my Ph.D. program in history. The investments from my trust have helped us to pursue our goals. My father continues to provide for me.

I am about to begin my thesis. My subject is the atrocities of World War II that most people have never heard about, as I had always intended, including the events in Oradour. I shall try in my thesis to explore the enormity of the war by writing about some of the forgotten incidents in which individual human beings, with names and faces and lives to be lived, with all that they had to contribute to the world, were lost to us.

Sophie loved the subject of my thesis. "The horrors of the Holocaust make people forget about the enormous tragedy of the war as a whole, that over fifteen million soldiers were killed, that an estimated forty-five million civilians died," she said. This was a generous statement from her, considering all that she and Steffa had suffered from the Final Solution.

Since my marriage, when asked where I come from in France, I answer Oradour. The name of the town means nothing. I watch the blank expression that my answer evokes for just a moment before I say, "A town near Limoges, in southwestern France, Bordeaux wine country," and the blank expression turns to a knowing smile. But they do not know.

I return to France once a year or so, sometimes lugging children, sometimes not. When Brian and I were married he promised me that he would make this possible and he has kept his word. I visit Mother Céline and the others in Fontvielle, I spend some time with Sophie and Steffa in Paris. I do not return to Oradour.

I went once to visit Colette in Limoges. Léon had sent me her address and her married name shortly before he died. I went on a weekday morning, when her husband was at work, her children at school. It was a difficult day for me. I did not know my friend. I did not recognize her as an adult, perhaps because I had no clear picture in my mind of her as a child. All I had ever remembered was the back of her, her braids flying, as she ran away from me on that infamous day. But she remembered me. "Oh, I'd know you anywhere, Christine, you are just the same," she said, and, not wanting to hurt her feelings, I pretended that my memory was just as good as hers. We told each other all about our present lives, showed each other pictures of our husbands, our children. "This is Christine," Colette said, showing me a photo of her only daughter. "Yes, I named her for you, my best friend. I did not know what had happened to you, but I never forgot you." I felt embarrassed, ashamed of my amnesia.

As Colette chattered on happily of the friendship we had shared as children, I just went along with everything she said and, in the end, she did rouse in me a few recollections that, lying dormant so many years, needed only a little prompting to come to the fore. I had had a dog named Toby, and I could suddenly see him, yellow and scruffy. My father had smoked a pipe, and yes, I could see him standing in a doorway, his face still indistinct, but, yes, he was puffing on his pipe, and I remembered, not the smell of his tobacco exactly, but how much I had loved the smell. Colette spoke of the time my brother Jean-Claude had broken his arm, and suddenly I remembered his fall from the tree and my mother carrying him to the house, Jean-Claude screaming as the doctor set the broken bone, how afraid I had been.

We spoke very little of the day the Germans came to Oradour. Colette, an only child, had lost her parents on that day, and she had lived the rest of her childhood with relatives in Limoges. "Will you tell your children about Oradour?" I asked. "Never," Colette answered emphatically. "I will never tell them. As far as they are concerned, my parents died of old age in their beds. I returned only once, for an assessment of my parent's property. I shall never return again, I shall never take my children there. I want only to forget." When I took my leave of Colette, I knew I would never come back, though we do keep in touch by mail from time to time.

I have had some more small memories of my life as a child in Oradour, but most are vague and blurry, scattered pictures. The strongest new images are of a forest, a thick canopy overhead with pinpoints of dappled sunlight, the damp, soft earth, wet leaves and broken twigs, sweet and earthy smells that evoke a feeling of serenity and well-being. I think the forest that I see must be where Colette and I had the secret hiding place she told me about, the forest that hid us from the Germans and saved our lives. I do love to walk in a forest whenever I have the chance. Like the sea, being surrounded by trees always calms my spirit and makes me feel safe. Other images, awake or asleep, are fleeting, the more I grasp at them, the more they slip away. Perhaps I have recovered from Oradour all that I can.

Sophie and Steffa are living in the apartment within an apartment at 18, avenue de la Motte Picquet. When I left, I asked Monsieur Bernac if they could have the place. He drew himself up to his full height, he looked down on me with his imperious attitude and said he couldn't give over the apartment to anyone without serious references. I told him that I would be their reference. He still looked dubious even though I had never thrown a noisy party or indulged in any unseemly behavior. Determined to have my way on this, I told him that Sophie and Steffa were Holocaust survivors, and he capitulated without further protest.

Sophie is working for a publishing company, Steffa has a part-time job in the neighborhood patisserie where I used to buy my favorite almond cake. Life is difficult, money is tight. The state pays for Steffa's medical care, and, as Jewish survivors of Nazi persecution, they hope eventually to receive compensation for their family home and possessions and for the wrong that was done to them when their country betrayed them. But Sophie wants to save this money, if it comes, for Steffa's future should she never truly recover from her experiences enough to make her own way in the world, as seems likely, and so they must be frugal.

Steffa is sometimes better, sometimes worse. She is now seeing a Paris psychiatrist, Maria Torok, whose methods for confronting psychic pain and trauma, for, as she says, liberating people from the phantoms that haunt their memories and limit their freedom, have been highly praised and have drawn many Holocaust survivors to her care. Steffa is now, occasionally, able to speak to Sophie of her experiences, and Sophie feels that her sister is much improved since seeing Dr. Torok, that her depressions are not as protracted and not as debilitating as they once were.

I take courage from Sophie and Steffa. As they go on with life, I do as well. Sophie tells me that Steffa loves the singing from the Bernac library, that the music seems to calm her spirit. When I am in Paris I always treat them to a concert as well as splendid, outrageous meals.

I try always to remember Sophie's words, that I shall find God in other people. I think she is right when my children come to me with their proud discoveries or their tearful hurts, as I see them grow and learn, when I watch them sleep. I think she is right when my husband comes through the door at the end of a long day and looks so grateful to see me even when I am harried and disheveled and cranky, weary from childcare and thesis problems. I think she is right when I watch Steffa's face as she listens to a symphony orchestra, when I see the joy on Sophie's face at my arrival after a long absence. If God is love, than He is with me still, though I do not acknowledge His presence, and I am blessed.

We used some of the trust money to bring Sophie and Steffa to America for a visit. They came one August, when the French have their month-long holiday. We bucked the crowds and ignored the heat to show them Boston, of course, and New York City, and Washington, D.C. Sophie wanted to see everything there was to see and ran us into complete exhaustion. Even Steffa exhibited more enthusiasm than I had ever seen in her. Next time they come we shall go west to see the great open spaces and the dramatic landscapes. We shall also have to find a cowboy or two because Sophie insists that we must. I'm sure Sophie went home and told all her friends every little detail about what she had seen in America and how marvelous she had found the country to be, boring some and infuriating others.

During Sophie's visit we had a chance to discuss the idea of collaborating on a book about France during the war. We are both excited about the prospect, and we plan to go ahead as soon as I have finished my thesis. Meanwhile, Sophie, energetic as ever, has been reading and doing research and interviewing people. I am anxious to join her. I knew she couldn't ignore the need for wartime truth.

I am usually too busy and too engaged to dwell on the events of my childhood in terms of my personal loss. As I work on my thesis, I have been able so far to remain removed and objective, the subject not belonging to me as an individual but to the entire world. I feel I must maintain this clinical approach if my thesis is to be a worthwhile endeavor.

Brian and I live an ostensibly religious life. We are, in most ways, a Roman Catholic family, we follow the traditions of my upbringing, of Brian's. Religious ritual can still leave me feeling unspeakably lonely, for the God I used to love and trust is still gone from me. Brian understands and he does not prod. I do not accept that the torment of doubt is a precious gift as the nuns had taught, and I do not want those I love to suffer such torment. Let them believe, believe absolutely. And so our children are being raised in the faith. Brian and I attend Mass regularly, I go for the sake of our children. I even take communion with Brian and our parish church is still standing. I do this in order to avoid questions I cannot answer from my daughter, who has just made her First Holy Communion.

Fire is still an issue, but since Mary Katherine's First Communion day, when a small, almost insignificant incident occurred, I am able to derive some pleasure from the warm light of candles on a dinner table or as festive Christmas decorations. As we were leaving church that day, Mary Katherine suddenly grabbed my hand. "Wait just a minute," she said, "I promised Sara Goldenberg I'd light a candle for her today.

They don't do that in her church, I guess, so she asked me to light one for her, that she will pass arithmetic. Otherwise, her parents are going to kill her."

We walked to the small chapel of Our Lady at the side of the main altar. Brian rummaged in his pocket for some coins which he dropped in the offering box to finance the candle for Sara Goldenberg. Mary Katherine picked up the taper, took the flame from one of the glowing candles and lit the votive for her friend Sara, that she should pass arithmetic, that her parents shouldn't kill her.

"You know what, this is such a special day, let's light all the candles," I said. "For the whole world."

"Oh, let's do," Mary Katherine said excitedly, and she picked up the long taper, took the flame from Sara Goldenberg's candle and began bringing all the other candles alive.

"The whole world," Brian said. "That's a pretty tall order. I guess I'd better ante up a little more cash." He took some bills from his wallet, folded them and crammed them through the little slit in the offering box.

When all the candles were aglow I stepped back to admire our handiwork. For the first time since I had been to Oradour, I looked at the flickering flames and I did not see fire. I saw light. When I looked at the face of my little girl, I saw only light reflected in her dark and happy eyes.

But it is still difficult for me when Brian sets the logs in the hearth ablaze, for then the flames are too big, too unrestrained, too unruly. They growl and crackle too loudly. But if I wait until the fire dies down a bit and keep my back to the fireplace, I can enjoy the warmth that is welcome in our old drafty house during the cold New England winters.

I try to remember what Léon told me, that as many people were killed by bullets as by fire. It is a small consolation but one I cling to. I pray every day, as though time has stopped in Oradour, as though it is still possible to affect the events of 1944, that my loved ones did not die by fire. It makes no sense, but still I pray for this small mercy.

Yes, I do still pray. I do not know if any creative or redemptive being hears my words or attends to my petitions, but still I pray. Habit? Hedging my bets? Both, I suppose. But more. The need for prayer that I was given as a child is as strong as ever, and I cry out from my mortal state of confusion and pain and fear and even anger, asking for strength and consolation from anyone with power over the universe who will listen. I pray as those I love most dearly, my family living, my family dead, have prayed. I pray to God the Father, to God the Son, to God the Holy Spirit, as I did throughout my childhood, for this is my tradition, these are the words I know. I pray to the Mother of Jesus Christ, for as much as I miss her Son I miss the maternal entity. If I do not believe in the loving Father or the sacrificial Son, the idea of the holy mediatrix seems absurd, and yet I pray to her, *Sancta Maria, mère de Dieu, priez pour nous.*

I pray to be forgiven for my sins, I pray for the well-being of those I love, I pray for the destitute and the despairing and the sick and the dying, I pray for the peace of the world. And I pray that my faith of old will be given back to me one day. Until then, I pray, not out my own faith, but out of the faith of those I love.

I also pray out of the faith of a woman I never knew, except through her children, in words that are not of my tradition, in words I did not know until now. I pray these words that Steffa taught to Sophie, who in turn taught them to me, the words of their lost mother's favorite prayer:

Lord, where shall I find thee?
High and hidden in thy place;
And where shall I not find thee?
The world is full of thy glory.

I have sought thy nearness,
With all my heart I called thee,
And going out to meet thee
I found thee coming toward me.

And then I pray in my own words that the faith reflected in this most beautiful prayer did not desert the suffering woman at the end and that somehow she knew two of her children would survive. I thank her for the gift to me of her two daughters—a kind of prayer in itself.

Out of my own personal faith, I pray, as well, every day, to the woman in the flowered dress eternally cutting beans into a pot. She remains with me, always, her dimpled, gap-toothed smile, her shining black eyes. She has not faded with the years. I treasure her face, the way she looks at me, with love. I treasure the love she evokes inside me. When I contemplate her face, I am not sorry I found my way to Oradour. If the horrific images I carried with me from that place are the price I must pay for the woman in the flowered dress, then the price is not so dear. Perhaps one day I shall have my children pay the same price, that they may know her. Perhaps the woman, my mother, is God made visible to me without my fully realizing it. Perhaps one day she will find a way to help me understand. As Saint Thomas had to touch the nail wounds, had to put his hand in the place where Jesus had been pierced with a lance before he would believe, perhaps I cannot believe unless I touch my mother's face, put my hand on the wound that killed her. And so without a miracle my apostasy continues. Do I, who doubt the existence of a loving God, believe in miracles? Can there be a miracle without a beneficent deity? I cannot get my mind around such a dilemma, I cannot do the logic. I only know that my mother is the key. My mother's death cost me my faith. Only my mother's life can give God back to me.

As one prays to a saint, I pray to my martyred mother, sanctified by blood, for the faith I possess now is in her. It is a living faith that supports my life. I believe in her goodness. I believe in her love. I believe in her intercession. Above all else, I believe in her suffering, that the grace she earned in the church in Oradour in 1944 is still operating in the world today, still operating within me. If I do not believe in grace, the spiritual force by which human suffering is transformed into eternal love and redemption, my family died for nothing, and this is a premise I shall not accept. And so I am a believer after all, as I pray the prayers I learned at my mother's knee, as I talk to her and ask her for strength and guidance. I believe she is with me for I see her, I feel her love. Perhaps one day my mother will step to one side of my vision and I shall see a loving God as well.

AFTERWORD

The following are but a few of the incidents of civilian
massacres in occupied lands during World War II. These
massacres occurred in response to Résistance activities but
became orgies of indiscriminate killing, including, in many
cases, the slaughter of women and children. The names of
the towns where these atrocities took place are mostly
unknown in the wider world. But the repercussions are still
being felt by the survivors—the relatives and friends of the
dead—and their descendants, whose feelings about the
world will always be tainted by these horrific events.

*Lidice, Czechoslovakia, June 10, 1942, 172 dead
Kortelisy, Ukraine, Russia, September 2, 1942,
   2,892 dead
Kalavryta, Greece, December 13, 1943, 1,300 dead
Bajki, Belarus, Russia, January 22, 1944, 987 dead

* The day of the Lidice massacre is the same, two years earlier, as the
massacre in Oradour-sur-Glane.

Ardeatine Caves, Rome, Italy, March 23, 1944,
355 dead

**Tulle, France, June 9, 1944, 99 dead

***Distomo, Greece, June 10, 1944, 218 dead

Sant'Anna di Stazzema, Italy, August 12, 1944,
560 dead

Maillé, France, August 25, 1944, 124 dead

Monte Sole, Italy, September 29–October 1, 1944,
1,830 dead

De Woeste Hoeve, The Netherlands, March 6, 1945,
117 dead

** The Tulle massacre was carried out by the troops from the same SS division that perpetrated the massacre in Oradour the following day.

*** The Distomo massacre took place on the same date, June 10, 1944, as the massacre in Oradour.

ACKNOWLEDGMENTS

I wish to thank Aggie and Peggy and Jill and Joanne and Pat and Geri and Evans whose friendship has kept me on the straight and narrow, plodding along year after year, filling the closet with book after book. All of our splendid journeys together replenished my spirit and made me laugh and kept me going and gave me wonderful copy. May we wander again together.

Thank you, Marcel, for giving me France.

A special gratitude to my editor Renée Sedliar, who took me on an unexpected journey, one I had all but accepted I would never make. She led me, with patience and kindness and wisdom, along a way unknown to me without scaring me to death. She nudged but she never shoved. She suggested but she never shouted. She demanded, softly, so that she never intimidated. She got me where I needed to be. Renée, I thank you for this book.